BARROOM BLOOD

★ ★ ★

Ted's features turned ugly. "I've had enough of you, Slater!"

He took two threatening steps toward Slater.

"Ted, you fool . . ." growled Ben Gault.

Slater saw the lamplight flash off the blade of the Bowie knife. Quicker than the eye, he grabbed his bottle of whiskey by the neck and spun. His right arm knocked Ted's knife-hand aside and the left brought the bottle around full-swing to smash the youngest Gault's face. The bottle shattered. Ted bounced off the bar, fell, rolled over. His hands covered his face. Blood trickled through the clawing fingers.

Joe Gault came out of his chair in a fast crouching spin. In that split second it occurred to Slater that Joe Gault meant to draw down on him. And he didn't have a chance in hell of beating the gunslinger . . .

Also by Dale Colter

The Regulator

Published by
HARPERPAPERBACKS

DALE COLTER

THE REGULATOR

DIABLO AT DAYBREAK

HarperPaperbacks
A Division of HarperCollins*Publishers*

This is a work of fiction. The characters, incidents, and dialogues are products of the author's imagination and are not to be construed as real. Any resemblance to actual events or persons, living or dead, is entirely coincidental.

HarperPaperbacks *A Division of* HarperCollins*Publishers*
10 East 53rd Street, New York, N.Y. 10022

Cover art by Miro

First HarperPaperbacks printing: February 1991

Printed in the United States of America

HarperPaperbacks and colophon are trademarks of HarperCollins*Publishers*

10 9 8 7 6 5 4 3 2

CHAPTER 1

SAM SLATER RODE STRAIGHT INTO TROUBLE.

Not just any old kind of trouble. Apache trouble. Slater had good reason to know that this was the worst kind.

The sudden flurry of distant gunshots caused him to climb rein leather and stop the lanky claybank he was riding. Behind him, at the back end of a lead rope, the dun mare halted and whickered. A blanket-wrapped body was draped belly-down across the saddle cinched to the dun.

Slater reckoned that the whicker was the mare's way of telling him that she wasn't too happy about stopping. On the other side of that hogback ridge was water. Water was something that Slater and the horses had been all day without.

The dun knew there was water on the other side of that rock-cluttered rise because she could smell it. Slater knew because he was as familiar with the desert hereabouts as any white man living.

Slater scanned the length of the ridge with narrowed eyes as ice-blue as a mountain lake in winter. On the far side were alkali flats rimmed with sierra. Snaking across the flats was an arroyo that stayed bone-dry except for a quarter-mile stretch where water came up out of springs, trickled downstream, and finally disappeared into the ground. The Mexicans called it Corto Agua; literally, "short water."

Whites called it Ghost Springs. Story was that, many years ago, a Mormon wagon train had made the mistake of trying to cross this part of the desert on its way to greener pastures farther west. They had relied on a Spanish land grant map over a hundred years old. That map had shown Corto Agua eight miles from its present location. Nobody knew for sure whether the mapmakers had erred or if Corto Agua had somehow vanished from one stretch of the arroyo and reappeared at some later date in a new location.

Failing to find water in the arroyo, the doomed

wagon train had pressed on. Most of its occupants had perished. Their oxen and horses dead of thirst, the Mormons had split up into groups and fanned out in all directions, looking for water.

Legend had it that their spirits still roamed the desert seeking those elusive springs.

Slater was familiar with the legend. He had no intention of joining the ranks of lost souls wandering this particular acre of hell in search of water. He had to get to Ghost Springs. There was no alternative open to him. In these parts, water was worth its weight in gold. The next reliable source was a day-and-a-half's ride away. And he had used up all the water he'd carried with him tracking down the owlhoot who was now draped cold-stone-dead across the dun mare.

Kicking the claybank into motion, Slater made for the base of the ridge, the dun and its grisly cargo in tow. As he rode, he listened with keen interest as the gunfire degenerated into a sporadic exchange of hot lead.

Dismounting, he tethered the claybank to the gnarled trunk of an ironwood twisting with stubborn will up through slabs of granite. He untied the lead rope from his saddlehorn and secured the dun to the tree, as well. Drawing a Spencer .56-50 rifle from his saddle boot, he thumbed the magazine cut-off just forward of the trigger guard. He removed a single rimfire cartridge from a loop at the back of his shellbelt, where he kept a few extra .56-50s for the Spencer, and fed the cartridge through the loading gate. That gave him the seven in the tubular magazine, plus one.

Taking the bandanna from around his neck, he wrapped it loosely around the rifle's receiver. This didn't interfere with the working of the lever or the ejection of spent casings. In fact, it caught the casings and saved Slater the time it took to pick them up. Brass cost money, and he made his own reloads. The bandanna served another purpose. The sun was blazing high in a sky bled of all color. Slater did not care to give himself away by carelessly flashing sunlight off the receiver.

His final precaution was to tie down the holster which held a Schofield .45 revolver. He had a steep climb through a jumble of rocks ahead of him; the last thing he wanted was the sidegun banging against stone.

He worked his way up through the boulders, agile and surefooted. He knew how to move, quick, silent and unseen, through all kinds of terrain. This was an ability essential to his dangerous trade.

Reaching the rim, he stayed low, peering through a narrow notch between two massive boulders of gray granite. The vista of the white flats spread out before him. In the far distance, mountains floated on a shimmering sliver of heat haze.

Much closer was the serpentine gash of the arroyo.
And hard by the arroyo was the adobe stage station
that marked the location of Ghost Springs.

In and around the stage station was where the
shooting was taking place.

Even at this distance Slater could see a drift
of gunsmoke from the stage station. The desert air
was clear as crystal, and his vantage point was su-
perb. The report reached him a second later. He
saw more smoke from two spots in front of the station, heard two more reports. Then he saw move-
ment. Someone running, zigzagging fleetly across
open ground, then disappearing into the deep cut
of the arroyo at the side of the station.

Slater grimaced. All he'd had time for was a
brief glimpse, but he was certain that the runner
was an Apache. An Apache was the last thing he
wanted to see.

After all, he knew Apaches. He had lived
among them for years.

He put two and two together. The reservation
was not far from here. Young broncos "jumping"
the agency and setting out on a little raiding spree
was a chronic problem. The Apaches were nomads
and warriors. Trying to keep them penned up was
like trying to stop the wind.

"You can't keep a good man down," Slater
murmured.

Like as not, they were hankering after horses.

What better place to find some than at a stage station? Slater remembered the layout—he had passed through on more than one occasion to fill his canteen at the springs. The horses were kept in a corral behind the station. The corral walls were adobe, eight feet high and more than a foot thick. The thinking was that this would deter Apache horse-thieving.

Trying to outwit an Apache, though, was an exercise in futility. Given the chance, they would moisten a section of the wall with water, then cut through the adobe with a rawhide thong. This required one man to go up and over and inside with one end of the thong. Slater had himself learned the technique from Apache tutors.

Certain conclusions were safe to draw. One was that the Apaches were in a hurry. Otherwise they would have waited until dark to attack the station. This in turn indicated that they were being pursued, in all likelihood by the cavalry, and they were willing to risk an assault in broad daylight to get horses. Once mounted they would head for Mexico, killing and raping along the way. Horse soldiers would have a hard enough time catching Apache raiders who were afoot. Once the Apaches were mounted, the bluecoats didn't have a prayer.

Slater's next conclusion was worrisome. If they were concerned with their backtrail, the

Apaches would surely have posted a lookout on some high vantage point.

A lookout who was keeping an eye peeled for cavalry dust would also have seen Slater's dust.

Slater stopped spectating the stage station shootout and began to scan nearby high ground. If the lookout wasn't sharing this same ridge, then he had to be on that rock-strewn hill to the north. The hill was higher than the ridge, and it sloped down closer to the stage station. There was a lot of saltbush and cholla among the rocks on the hill, providing splendid cover.

"Ten to one you're up there, *hesh-ke*," said Slater.

He could only hope that such was the case, since he had come up on the backside of the ridge, which meant the lookout had seen his dust but probably hadn't seen him.

Slipping back down the slope to the horses, Slater tried to put himself in the Apache lookout's place. The Indian's job was to signal his brothers down below if he spotted trouble. The signal might be an agreed-upon number of rifle shots. More likely it would be with sun off metal or mirror. Rifles could jam at the most inconvenient times and cartridges were too valuable to waste on the sky.

The other Apaches were still trying to take the stage station, so the signal hadn't been given. The lookout would know that the dust he had seen wasn't the cavalry pursuit, that it had come from only one or two horses.

By the time he reached the scant shade of the ironwood, Slater had come up with a plan.

He didn't like the situation, but he felt it necessary to deal himself in. Not that he gave a tinker's damn about the person or persons fighting for their lives in the stage station. He wasn't moved to fight other folk's battles. Out here, every man was responsible for his own bacon.

No, his need and his reason was water. He had to get to it. He wasn't going to sit around and wait for the fight to end, because the lookout knew about him.

He had come this way for the water in Ghost Springs. By God, he was going to get some. The Apaches just happened to be in his way.

That was their hard luck.

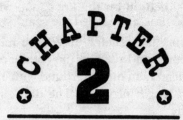

CHAPTER 2

SLATER FIGURED THAT THE LOOKOUT would think twice before leaving his post to investigate, that he would prefer to wait until Slater came into view before deciding on a course of action. Normally, the bronco left behind as lookout or horse-holder was the youngest and the least battle-tested. He would be anxious to prove himself, and wouldn't want to make a mistake. Slater hoped that was true in this case. He needed all the edge he could get.

The dead man was lashed down over the saddle with a rope that was looped around his knees, carried under the dun's barrel, looped again around his chest, dallied around the saddlehorn, and finally tied off on the knee loop with a clove hitch.

Working fast, Slater undid the hitch, shook out the loops, and pitched the corpse off the saddle. The dead man hit the ground with all the flexibility of a length of wood. The dun snorted and shied away.

"*Ho-shuh,*" whispered Slater. "*Ho-shuh.*"

The dun mare got quiet, watching him. The Apache horse talk worked to calm her down.

At six feet tall and then some, Slater carried his two hundred pounds of grit and muscle on a deceptively lean frame. He had no trouble hoisting the corpse back onto the saddle, this time in a seated position. He wasn't bothered by handling a dead body, even one such as this, whose clothes were caked black with dried blood. Dead bodies were Slater's stock-in-trade.

Keeping up the soft-spoken horse talk, Slater lashed the dead man's ankles to the stirrups and bound his wrists to the saddle's biscuit with piggin strings. He drew an old Colt sidehammer rifle from the saddle scabbard. Sliding the barrel under the dead man's waistband in the small of the back, Slater used the rifle as a brace against the spine, looping the rope a few times around the chest. Rigor mortis was a help rather than a hindrance at this point. The upper torso of the corpse was rigid, and would not slump.

The blanket that had once served as shroud now became a serape. Slater used his clasp knife to slash a foot-long slit in the center of it, threw it over the dead man's head and pulled it down to cover the rifle-brace and the blood.

Slater stepped back to examine his handiwork with a critical eye. He had worked fast, using up less time than it took to smoke a roll-your-own. He absently ran his thumb along the jagged scar that reached from his sideburn to the left corner of his thin-lipped mouth. The white scar tissue was prominent against the flat, bronze plain of his cheek.

He had to hope that, at a distance, the Apache lookout would be fooled into believing that the dead man was alive.

Slater figured to draw the lookout into the open and kill him. Then he could scatter the Apaches on the flats with some well-placed rifle fire from the hilltop.

One final touch was needed. He stepped in and reached up to plant his low-brimmed campaign hat on the dead man's head. He pulled it down low over the sightless, staring eyes, tightened the chin-strap under the jaw.

"Don't you go running off, Bitteroot," Slater said. "Your mangy hide's worth five hundred dollars to me, and I'm so broke I couldn't sit in one hand at a penny-ante poker game."

Unhitching the dun from the ironwood, Slater looped the reins around the dead outlaw's wrists, stepped back, and gave the mare a dust-raising whack on the rump.

The dun lit out at a canter. Slater was confident that the smell of water would draw the mare in the right direction. The way of least resistance led through a notch between ridge and hill, and the dun was heading that way.

Picking up the Spencer, Slater set out at a ground-eating lope.

Unlike most men who spent a lifetime on horseback, he was a good runner, thanks to his Apache training; he had the lungs and the leg muscles.

At first, he ran away from the ridge and adjacent hill. He found a drywash that angled off in the direction he wanted. He loped down it, completely hidden from anyone positioned on or near the crest of the hill.

His clothes, a plain white shirt and gray trousers of durable cavalry twill, blended well with the colors of the desert. His footwear—Apache *n'deh b'keh,* moccasins that laced up to the knee—made no noise. He kept to rocky ground as much as possible, raising no dust.

Where the drywash came nearest the slope of

the hill he climbed out and ducked quickly into a small stand of wolfberry. Somewhere in the rocks to his right a rattler gave its sinister warning. Slater ignored it, searching the slope above for any sign of Apache presence. An Apache was ten times as deadly as a diamondback.

Seeing nothing, he began the climb. He stayed low and moved fast, never taking more than ten strides at a time before finding cover. Every time he stopped, he crabbed to one side or the other a foot or two. Then he would wait and listen and search the rocky rim above him. And each time he made a move, it was at a different angle. He did not take a careless step or make a telltale sound. He was an expert in the art of manhunting. He had made a fair living at it for years.

Some said that Sam Slater was the best bounty hunter in the business.

The clatter of iron-shod hooves drifted on the still, hot air from the notch to his left. Reaching the cover of a jumble of granite boulders, he could look down and see the dun mare working through the rock rubble of the notch. The carcass of the notorious road agent known as Bitteroot Carson was still firmly lashed upright in the saddle. The going was rough for the mare, but she was making her way resolutely towards the flats, guided by the sweet scent of water.

Slater crouched among the boulders and

again scanned the slope in front of him. If his ruse worked, the lookout would come down from the crest to get a closer look at the dun and its cargo—a closer look, or a better shot.

But he saw nothing.

The shooting out on the flats suddenly stopped.

Slater looked to the crest in time to see the flash of sun on the receiver of a rifle. The lookout was signaling; the Apaches were breaking off the attack on the stage station. Why? Because of the approach of what the lookout thought was a lone rider? Slater turned and checked the desert behind him. He immediately saw the thick plume of dust. Many horses, at least five miles away. Cavalry, he guessed. Riding to the sound of gunfire.

This new development forced Slater to change his tactics. The Apaches were going to make a run for it. He didn't have to tangle with them now. Better to slip back to his horse. By that time it would be safe to recover Bitteroot's valuable carcass and ride on in to the springs.

He took two steps away from the boulders and heard the bullet whine off rock and buzz angrily past him, too close for comfort. Diving back to cover, he flinched as another bullet smacked into the granite that sheltered him.

The lookout was shooting at him from the crest of the hill.

Smiling bleakly, Slater wiped sweat out of his eyes.

So much for trying to sneak up on an Apache.

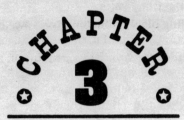

CHAPTER 3

THE SAFEST COURSE OF ACTION WAS TO stay down low behind the rocks. Time was running out for the Apache raiders. The cavalry was riding to the rescue. This time, at least, they weren't a day late and a dollar short. And the contingent of horse soldiers wasn't a small one. The size of the distant dust cloud was evidence of that.

The fact that he was pinned down by a solitary bronco, and that he had failed to reach the top of the hill unseen, despite his best effort, didn't bother Slater or do damage to his pride. He knew better than to underestimate an Apache.

So he braced his back against a tall slab of

rock and settled back to wait it out. Discretion was the better part of valor.

When he heard the clatter of loose rocks avalanching down-slope far to his right, he changed his mind.

The lookout was descending the hill and making for the notch below. Slater chanced a cautious look around the clump of boulders concealing him. He saw the Indian and brought the Spencer to his shoulder—only to lower the rifle, astonished by what he saw.

The Apache wasn't alone. There was a woman with him.

Slater saw the long, tousled blond hair and knew that she was a white woman. A prisoner. Her hands were bound in front of her. The bronco was pulling her roughly along behind him, with a good grip on a short length of rope that was secured to the bindings on her wrists. At a distance of about two hundred feet, with all the rock and brush between them, Slater caught only glimpses of them both. But he saw her stagger and fall, unable to keep up the pace. Then the Apache turned and kicked her savagely, trying at the same time to hoist her to her feet.

Slater again whipped stock to shoulder. This time he fired. Just as he did, the Indian moved, and the shot was wasted. The woman was on her feet now, and the Apache hauled her out of Slater's sight. Slater swore under his breath and commenced running downhill, at an angle that would take him closer to his prey. As he ran he levered another round into the breech.

Dodging thorny cholla and crashing through a four-foot-high stand of rabbitbrush, Slater went up and over a rib of granite, heard the shot and in reflex fell backward. The rifle spoke a second time, a flat crack. He couldn't see the Indian, but he was certain that the Apache was the one doing the shooting.

This time, though, the shots weren't aimed at Slater. Down in the notch, a horse uttered a shrill whinny. A heartbeat later, he saw the dun mare trot into view below. The mare was going back the way it had come, away from the flats and the water. The bronco had turned it with a well-placed shot or two.

Twice more the Apache fired. Slater could clearly see the puff of dust rise from the blanket serape draped over Bitteroot Carson's shoulders. The slug's impact shoved the corpse sideways in the saddle. The second bullet smacked into rock directly in the mare's path and screamed away. Snorting, the dun careened sideways and tried to go up the far side of the notch, but the way was too steep. The horse came back down and began to fiddlefoot, uncertain what to do or which way to go, and getting no guidance from the dead man lashed firmly to its back.

"You clever bastard," said Slater, powering to his feet.

As he had feared, the lookout had a good reason for descending into the notch, so well within range of Slater's rifle, instead of taking a safer, more roundabout route.

The Apache was after the dun mare. With some excellent shooting, he was trying to keep the horse penned in the notch until he could get down to her. He had put one, probably two, bullets into Bitteroot's carcass, unaware that he was trying to kill a corpse. Slater reckoned he was more than a little perplexed by his failure to shoot the rider of the dun out of the saddle. But that wasn't going to stop the Indian.

Slater heard another cascade of loose rock, and realized that this was the woman who was being so clumsy, as captor and captive continued their reckless descent.

Slater took off running again. He had to protect his investment. That dun had been Bitteroot's cayuse, and Slater had hoped to fetch seventy or eighty dollars for her, throwing in the tack and the old Colt sidehammer of the desperado to sweeten the deal. He did not intend to make the bronco a gift of all that.

He was almost to the bottom of the hill, and

charging headlong around a jumble of boulders, when he saw the Indian and the woman again, below and to his right a scant fifty yards, out in the open on a broad shoulder of granite. The Apache saw him at the same instant. The woman prevented Slater from having a clear shot. The bronco spun, holding his rifle one-handed, and tugged sharply on the rope with the other, trying to pull the woman in front of him, intending to use her as a shield.

Slater had a split second to make his decision. It was kill or be killed. There was no time to stop running. No time to find cover. To live, he had to put the Apache down for good. And to accomplish that he had to shoot through the woman.

The Indian fired.

Letting go of the Spencer, Slater pitched forward. He heard the bullet's passage. It was that close. What saved him was the fact that the Apache was firing on the move, one-handed, and at hip-level.

As Slater fell, the woman collided with the Indian. She was falling, too, and struck the Apache across the legs. They both went down and rolled twenty feet before stopping. The Indian bounced up. The woman lay still, face-down. Letting go of the rope, the Apache whirled to face Slater, working the lever action of the repeater, wanting to put another bullet into the bounty hunter. Slater's fall had almost convinced him that his last shot had hit home, but he wanted to put one more into Slater, just to be safe.

This time, the Indian spent an extra second or two taking careful aim at the moving target.

That was his first—and last—mistake.

Slater came out of the rolling descent with the Schofield .45 in hand. The woman was out of the way. He had a clear shot now. He fanned the hammer, running straight at the bronco. All three bullets hit the mark. The Apache was hurled backwards, the rifle flying out of his grasp. He rolled past the woman and into a stand of cholla.

Slater loped past the woman without sparing her a glance. His attention was riveted to the Indian. As he drew closer to the Apache, he fired once more, putting a bullet into the base of the skull. Only then was he satisfied that his adversary was dead. A man could not be too careful; Apaches were damned hard to kill.

Kneeling, he rolled the Indian over. The Apache had not seen many summers. Hardly more than a boy, but still and all, a lean and wiry desert wolf, garbed in a brown hickory shirt, breechclout, and *n'deh b'keh*, with a gunbelt strapped around his waist. Slater took a pistol from the flap holster. This was an old war-vintage Griswold cap-and-ball, its brass frame rusted. It was of dubious value. Slater tossed it away.

Looking down at the young Apache, he felt no satisfaction and no remorse. He did what he had to do in order to survive. He killed when he had to kill, without second thought.

He had to give the dead bronco high marks for gumption. The young warrior had kept a good lookout for his brothers, and fought well against Slater. He had done his utmost to keep the woman prisoner and at the same time tried to acquire the dun mare. Success would have brought him great honor.

Slater rose, listened for a moment. No more gunfire from the stage station. He could not see down onto the flats from here, but he felt confident that the rest of the Apache raiders were long gone.

Going to the woman, he gently rolled her over onto her back. She was out cold. Her brown riding skirt and white blouse were torn and soiled. Her feet were bare and bleeding, her arms and legs covered with scratches and bruises. Hair the color of cornsilk was tangled and matted with blood. A nasty-looking gash at the hairline was bleeding profusely. Beneath all the blood, bruises, and dirt, she was an attractive young woman.

All the injuries Slater could see were superficial. Given a little time and treatment, they would heal. He wasn't so sure about the *other* wounds, the ones you couldn't see. He could well imagine what she had been through during her captivity.

Those inner scars would be slow to fade, if they faded at all.

He felt no outrage, as other less-hardened men might have, upon seeing a woman so abused. The desert was a brutal place, populated by brutal men. Out here, life tended to be short, dirty, and violent.

Holstering the Schofield, Slater climbed up the slope to retrieve his rifle. He also found the Apache's long gun, a Winchester repeater. This was a weapon worth recovering.

The bandanna wrapped loosely around the Spencer's receiver now served to tie both weapons to his shellbelt, so that they hung down by his leg. This done, he lifted the unconscious woman effortlessly in his arms, and carried her down into the notch.

CHAPTER 4

SLATER WAS AROUND THE BACK OF THE
stage station, in the corral and reading sign, when
he heard the cavalry approaching.

The corral was attached to the station building, so that one could step out the back door and
into it, or could see into it through the single rear
window. A heavy, timbered gate, reinforced with
strap iron, was set into the rear wall of the corral,
and led to a steep path descending into the arroyo
and to the sweet, clear water produced by the
springs. The gate was too sturdy to force, and the
Apaches had cut into the adobe of the wall.

There had been two stage company employees

present at the station at the time of the attack. One had been killed with the first shot. The other had been unable to watch the corral and at the same time keep the Apaches at bay in front.

Slater stepped through the gap cut out of the adobe and circled to the front of the station, slipping into the striped shade of the picket overhang as the column of horse soldiers arrived in a choking drift of alkali dust.

They did not arrive in fancy parade-ground formation. There were no column-by-twos or crisp by-the-book commands or sharp wheeling into line. These troopers were caked with dust and sweat, riding horses that were close to bottomed-out. A single glance was enough to assure Slater that these men were seasoned veterans. And they were all black men, with the exception of the captain in the lead and the two Coyotero scouts flanking him. Tenth Cavalry "buffalo soldiers"; good men in a fight. A red-and-white guidon indicated that this was at least a portion of that celebrated regiment's D Company.

At first, only the captain and one of the Apache scouts dismounted. The others stayed in their McClellan saddles. Slater took a quick head count and came up with a total of twenty-five, including the Coyoteros.

The captain stepped stiffly into the shade of the overhang, glanced at Slater, then at the two bodies laid out in the dust near the front door of the station. One was the slain stage company employee. The other was the outlaw, Bitteroot Carson, whom Slater had removed from the dun mare, now tethered with the claybank at the tie rail a few strides away.

"Apaches do this?" asked the officer.

Slater pointed with his chin at the body of the stage company man. "They did that. I did the other."

The captain gave Slater a close study. He saw a tall man, wide in the shoulder, narrow in the hips. Wheat-colored hair was lank and long, chiseled features were covered with a dark stubble of beard. The nose had been broken at least once. A jagged scar was prominent on his left cheek. He had the look of a man who was not only a product of the desert, but also a part of it.

Slater returned the once-over. The officer was a gaunt, craggy-faced individual with piercing, sun-washed eyes and a close-cropped beard. He wore a black slouch hat and a plain blue tunic with the captain's bars displayed on shoulder straps. Slater sensed that this man was no novice. Perhaps once, long ago, he had put his trust in *Cooke's Cavalry Tactics*; by now, the law of desert survival and Apache warfare had taught him a whole new set of rules.

He also knew his lessons in frontier etiquette.

He did not demand an explanation. He did not require Slater to identify himself. In fact, he did not give a tinker's damn about Slater or the dead hombre Slater claimed as his own kill. His job was to apprehend rampaging Apaches.

"They came for horses," he reasoned. "Did they get any?"

"All of 'em," was Slater's reply.

A grimace tightened the captain's features. His worst fear had been realized.

"Then I have as much chance of catching them as I would finding a horse thief in heaven."

"Go back to Fort McDowell, Captain," advised Slater.

"I have my orders. I am in the habit of obeying them."

The captain turned. The Coyotero scout still mounted nodded understanding as the officer held up a forefinger and made a curt circular motion. The Apache rode out of the station yard and into the sagebrush.

"They headed west," Slater mentioned, knowing that the scout had been dispatched to reconnoiter the area and discover the direction of the Apaches' flight. "There were eight of them. One was wounded, but not seriously. Six of them had rifles. They stole twelve horses, including one that's slightly lame. They'll kill that one for food before the day is out."

The captain scrutinized him even more closely now. There was no question that this tall, soft-spoken desert rider knew what he was talking about. Obviously he had scouted the area himself prior to the arrival of the column.

"Well, that's great," muttered the captain darkly. "So they've got food and mounts and rifles. And water, of course."

"I reckon," nodded Slater.

The other Coyotero was giving the front wall of the stage station a careful examination. Taking a knife from his army-issue web belt, he dug a spent slug out of the adobe. He removed several more bullets in this manner, studying each one. Slater figured he was trying to get a handle on what kind of weapons the raiders were armed with. Having done his own investigating, and finding shell casings in the arroyo and out on the flat surrounding the station, Slater already had a pretty good idea what kind of firearms the broncos possessed. But he offered no more information. The Coyotero was getting paid to do what he was doing—let him earn his keep.

The captain called for his first sergeant. This noncom brought his horse forward. He was an older man; the short-cropped hair under his forage cap was dusted with gray. His mount, noticed Slater, was lathered from stem to stern and looked about ready to drop in its tracks.

"Detail pickets, sergeant," said the captain. "Get those horses watered. The stage company kept their teams grain-fed, so we should be able to find some feed for these nags. And have the men fill their canteens at the springs."

"Yessuh, Cap'n."

The sergeant reined the horse around and began bellowing orders in a voice that cracked like a freighter's bullwhip. The troopers dismounted. Several gathered up all the canteens and headed for the arroyo. A half-dozen more, under a corporal's supervision, took charge of the horses and began taking them to water by turns. Two went in search of grain. Pairs struck out in four different directions to post themselves in the desert some distance from the station. The sergeant sent two more inside to find a way up onto the flat roof. As they went past him, Slater took a close look at the carbines this pair carried. They were breech-loading .45/70 "Trapdoor" Springfields. Fine weapons, mused the bounty hunter, possessed by men who knew how to shoot. Too bad for them that they'd likely never draw a bead on a single bronco this time out.

After the two troopers entered the station, another man emerged. He was a big, brawny character with an unkempt red beard and beady, mud-brown eyes. He wore a wide-awake hat, a red flannel shirt and serge trousers tucked into trapper's boots. A Remington Navy Model revolver was belted to his side. He carried a Sharps-Borschardt hammerless rifle in one meaty fist and a warbag in the other.

Seeing the Coyotero gave him a bad start. He dropped the warbag and swung the rifle up. The captain stepped in swiftly to grab the barrel and push down.

"Look again, Taggert. He's with me."

The man named Taggert had a wad of shag tobacco bulging in one cheek. Now he spat a stream of brown juice against the adobe wall of the station, a demonstration of contempt for all Apaches, be they Army scouts or no.

"Well, if it ain't Captain Mack," said Taggert. "You missed the shindig, Captain."

"What happened?"

"What d'you think? Look around. Damned red savages killed poor Bantry here and made off with the stock. I'm just lucky to be alive. Bantry went down with the first shot. They was just lyin' out there waitin' for one or both of us to stick our fool necks out. It was all I could do to keep 'em from bargin' in through the front door. Whilst they kept me busy, a couple cut through the corral wall and took the horses. They can have 'em. They can have the whole kit and caboodle, far as I'm concerned. I'm dustin' out of this country for good."

"Where are you going?" Captain Mack glanced at the warbag.

"Hard of hearin', Captain?" Taggert was scared and angry and in no mood to be civil. "I quit. I never shoulda let the company talk me into transferring down here to this Godforsaken territory in the first place. Up Montana way, where I hail from, at least the redskins come at you out in the open. These damned 'Paches—you never see 'em until they're killing you. Sneakin' yellow-bellied bastards."

"I don't have a horse to spare for you, Taggert," said Mack. "You're better off staying here than you are taking off on foot."

"Town's only twenty miles east. The 'Paches headed west. I ain't stayin' here another damned minute." Taggert looked at the body of his co-worker, Bantry. "I'll let you bury the dead, Captain. You might as well take your own sweet time about it, too. You blueboys never do catch those copperbellies anyhow, do you?"

"I'm heading for that town," said Slater. "You can go with me, if you don't mind riding double with a dead man."

"I do mind," said Taggert, truculent. "You're a bounty hunter, ain't you? I knowed it the minute I seen you riding in. I don't want nothin' to do with a bounty man. I'd rather walk."

Slater shrugged. "Suit yourself." He was used

to hostility from strangers. Many of the men who came west did so to escape past misdeeds, and they were wary of lawmen and bounty hunters.

Captain Mack glanced at the body of Bitteroot Carson, then at Slater, comprehension dawning in his eyes.

Taggert brushed past them, out into the blinding heat beyond the shade of the picket overhang, only to pause and turn to face them.

"And as for that woman you done brought in, bounty man, my advice is to cut her throat. That would be mercy, not murder, in my book. You can see she's been used, and used hard, by those sons of bitches. Like as not, she'll want to kill herself when she comes to and realizes what all's been done to her. I've seen it before. You'd be doing her a favor."

With that, he walked away.

"Woman?" muttered Captain Mack. "What woman?"

"The Apaches had a lookout up on that rise, yonder," explained Slater. "He saw my dust, so I had to kill him. He had a woman captive with him. I brought her here."

"My God, man! Where is she?"

"Inside."

Mack charged through the doorway. Slater followed, heard the Coyotero scout coming behind him, and turned to block the entrance.

"Dah," he said bluntly. "No. Stay out."

Captain Mack said, "Santos is my scout. I'll thank you not to give orders to my men."

"Think about it, Captain," urged Slater, trying to be reasonable. "If she comes to and sees an Apache standing over her, after what's happened, do you reckon she'll care what side he's on?"

"I see your point." Mack nodded to the Coyotero, who impassively returned to his scrutiny of the bullet-riddled adobe wall.

The stage station's "common" room was dark; the heavy, wooden shutters were still secured over the windows. Sunlight lanced through the narrow gunslots cut into the shutters. Captain Mack quickly surveyed the room, with its long trestle table and benches, stone fireplace, and one wall covered with harnesses, draped on wooden pegs driven into the adobe. The floor was hardpacked earth.

Failing to find the woman he sought in this room, Captain Mack strode to a doorway draped with burlap, old grain sacks sewn together to make a curtain. Slater followed him into this second, smaller room, containing bunk beds and a small table crowned by a tin washbasin. Pages torn from a Montgomery Ward catalog and illustrations removed from the *Harper's Illustrated Weekly* half-covered the walls, secured with horseshoe nails.

Still unconscious, the blond woman lay on the

cornhusk mattress which covered the lower bunk. Slater had thrown a brown woolen blanket over her from the shoulders down.

"My God," breathed Mack. "It's her."

"Who?"

"That's Miss Amanda Woodbine. She was abducted three days ago. It was her ill fortune to have been present at the agency when the Apaches jumped the reservation. They began their rampage by killing the Indian agent and a couple of other men, and kidnapping Miss Woodbine."

"Woodbine?"

"Name ring a bell?" Mack smiled ruefully. "She happens to be the daughter of the territorial governor."

"I'll be damned."

"You'll be a hero, is what you'll be."

"I'll pass. There's no profit in it."

"There may be, this time. Prior to leaving the garrison, I received word that Governor Woodbine was offering a five-thousand dollar reward for the head of the Apache who led the breakout and massacre at the agency. Real troublemaker, name of Chacon. Since there's a bounty, maybe you'd be interested."

"Five thousand dollars." The words sounded good to Slater, but he had a sour taste in his mouth as he spoke them. "I never walked away from that kind of money. I reckon there's a first time for everything." He fixed cold, ice-blue eyes on the captain. "You take the woman back. Tell 'em you saved her, and leave me all the way out of it. I want no more part of this, if Chacon's involved."

"I judged you to be a man who's afraid of nothing and no one," remarked the officer. "But you sound afraid when you speak Chacon's name."

"Only a fool's unafraid of Apaches." Slater made to leave, but paused in the doorway. "I know Chacon, Captain. I know just how good a fighter he is. And how bad he can be. He's the only man I know who's better than I am. And worse."

CHAPTER 5

SLATER KEPT HIMSELF APART FROM THE troopers of D Company. Not because he had anything against them, he just had a lot on his mind, and was by temperament a loner.

Primarily due to Amanda Woodbine's presence and condition, Captain Mack gave orders that the column would stay at the stage station until dawn tomorrow. That made sense to Slater. Mack's assignment was to catch Chacon's band of raiders and rescue the governor's daughter. Thanks to Slater, he had accomplished half of his mission.

Slater would have bet a dollar—had he a dollar to his name—that Mack was not going to accomplish the other half. No matter how hard and how far he pushed his tough, resilient "buffalo soldiers," or how long he rested and watered and grained his horses.

The captain was assuming that, come morning, Miss Woodbine would be in condition to ride. He had arranged for the first sergeant and three of the married troopers to escort her to the town of San Manuel, which was closer than Fort McDowell, and which was where, apparently, Governor Woodbine could be found. The Coyotero scout, Santos, would provide his horse for the woman and proceed with the main column on foot. That was no hardship for an Apache if he was worth his salt. An Apache could run all day and keep pace with horses at the canter.

The troopers used the station's hearth to build a cookfire and heat a kettle of beans to go with their hardtack and coffee. Slater walked his claybank and the dun mare to the springs, found some grain for them, then settled down with his back to the rear wall of the corral, away from D Company. From here he could look down into the arroyo and behold the pleasing sight of clear, blue water in deep limestone pools.

He didn't pay much attention to the scenery, though. He was thinking about Taggert and Chacon.

Slater's past was coming back strong to haunt him.

Taggert's comment about hailing from Montana had started it. Slater touched the scar on his cheek. He had received that wound in a knife fight with his uncle, a prominent Montana rancher. Slater had become his uncle's ward after the murder of his parents by Indians.

Slater remembered his uncle as a man changed for the worse by the death of his wife. A man who, more and more, had come to rely on whiskey to blunt the pain of loneliness. Fifteen at the time, Slater had not felt obliged to interfere when his uncle embarked on his popskull binges. Personal tragedy affected different men in different ways. Some, like Slater, were toughened. Others, like Slater's uncle, were broken.

But the night that his uncle made drunken advances on his own daughter—Slater's cousin Lucinda—Slater *had* interfered. He had killed his uncle in self-defense. The cattleman had been bigger and stronger and kill-crazy, blinded by rage and rye whiskey.

Self-defense, sure and certain. Problem was, Montana didn't see it that way. Accused of murder, Slater fled south, a price on his head.

Out from the shadow of the hangman's noose Slater had run, into the desert Southwest. Out of the frying pan and into the fire. He had been cap-

tured by a renegade party of Bedonkohe Chiricahua. By all rights, Slater should have died a
horrible, lingering death. Yet the fierce old *nan-
tan*, Loco, had spared his life. Loco had just lost
one of his sons. He saw promise in the scrappy,
yellow-haired *Pinda-Lickoyi* youngster.

Loco had become like a father to Slater. The
old war-chief was stern but fair with his adopted
white-eyes son. Slater had grown to love the wild
life high in the sierra with the renegade Bedonkohe. Taught the Apache way of hunting and
fighting and tracking, he was a quick student.

He acquired many Apache habits, and was
guided by Apache likes and dislikes. He never ate
fish—in fact, the aroma of cooking fish turned his
stomach. He believed the bear to be a sacred animal. And, to this day, he considered mule meat a
delicacy.

With the exception of Loco, none of the Bedonkohe fully accepted him. They were civil, and
respected his prowess as a hunter and a fighter,
but he was always an outsider. So when Loco was
slain in a cavalry ambush, Slater had severed the
ties that bound him to the Chiricahua Apache, and
struck out on his own.

Bounty-hunting was a logical line of work for
Slater, considering where his talents lay. There
was always plenty of business. It was the perfect

career for a loner who had few equals when it came to manhunting and mankilling.

He, a wanted man, preyed on other wanted men. The irony of the situation did not elude him. The desert was a long way from Montana; still, looking over his shoulder had become habit.

This was the reason he kept thinking about Taggert.

Conceivably, Taggert had recognized him. Ten years had passed since that fight with his uncle. Slater had no idea if the "paper" on him was still circulating in Montana, and he had no idea how long Taggert had lived up there.

But he never underestimated anybody. And he never took unnecessary chances.

Which was the reason he had offered Taggert a ride to San Manuel. Slater was no good samaritan. He had simply wanted to keep the man in sight, until satisfied one way or the other.

Sitting there in the scant shade of the adobe wall, he moved not an inch as a woman's scream rent the still, furnace-hot afternoon. The scream was followed by muted sobbing.

A few minutes later, Captain Mack circled the corral and hunkered down near Slater. His features were grim.

"Miss Woodbine has regained consciousness." Mack's tone was hollow.

"So I heard."

"We're going after them at first light. Thought maybe you'd like to come along."

"You thought wrong."

"I also thought you might want to make them pay for what they did to that young woman."

"Get off your high horse, Captain. Your soldiers have been known to do the same thing to Apache women."

"No trooper under my command has . . ."

"Forget it."

Mack got a grip on his temper. "I could use your help. You obviously know the Apache. And you know your way around out here. I'll pay you a scout's wages."

"You've got scouts."

Mack made no reply. Slater smiled drily.

"Don't trust your Coyoteros, Captain?"

"To a point, yes."

Slater couldn't blame the cavalry officer for having reservations about his scouts. Some were capable, a few even reliable. Too many, though, were thieves and drunkards, spurned by their own people and treated with contempt by the army they served.

After a moment of moody silence, Mack said, "That man you killed. Outlaw?"

Slater nodded.

"Then I assume you'll be taking him into San Manuel."

"That's right."

"Then you could at least travel with the detachment escorting Miss Woodbine."

"Aren't you afraid the company of a bounty hunter and a day-old corpse might offend the lady?"

"I believe she would prefer that to falling into the hands of Chacon and his band again."

"She'll be safe enough. Chacon's got horses now, and he'll head for the high sierra. He won't double back."

"Sounds to me like you know how he thinks."

"Pretty much," allowed Slater.

"Then, for God's sake, help me get him. Before he kills any more men, or violates any more women."

Slater stood up. The sun was right behind him, red as fresh blood, nearing the western horizon. Mack had to squint up at the manhunter, and could not make out his expression. Slater's voice was hard as gunmetal.

"You're right, Captain. I know the Apache. I lived among them for a number of years. My Apache father was Loco, of the Bedonkohe. He was cut to pieces with sabers when your bluecoats ambushed the band. That was after he surrendered. I won't scout for the army against any Apache. Especially Chacon. Not that he and I are friends. He'd cut my throat quick as any other white man's. Maybe quicker."

"Then what is it about him?"

Slater drew a long breath.

"He's Loco's son. In a way, that makes Chacon my brother."

CHAPTER 6

SLATER LEFT THE STAGE STATION IN THE uncertain light of false dawn. He could have easily slipped past the pickets unseen, but he went out of his way to make his presence known. There was nothing to be gained by getting the troopers who stood watch in trouble with their commanding officer.

He kept to the stage road until sunrise. The sign of a white man on foot was clear in the alkali dust. Taggert. Making straight for San Manuel on the path of least resistance. That didn't mean, though, that he wouldn't circle back and lay in wait for Slater. His Sharps-Borschardt was a good rifle for long-range killing. Had he recognized Slater's face from a wanted poster seen long ago in Montana? If so, he looked the type to try his hand at a little bounty hunting of his own.

Slater decided to play it safe. Leaving the trace, he cut north across the sagebrush flat. In an hour he reached rough country which provided better cover. He kept to the high ground as much as possible. If Taggert was after him, he would not give the man the advantage of the high ground.

It was tough going. Much of the time he had to dismount and lead the horses. He stopped often, listening and looking, and paying attention to the claybank. The horse was a savvy animal, and every bit as good as a watchdog.

The bounty hunter knew this country well. He could keep to the hills all the way into San Manuel. The route was twice as long, but half as risky, as the stage road. On the road, he could reach town by early afternoon. He planned instead to take all day and go carefully through country that would be difficult for a man on foot. He would not give Taggert an easy target. It occurred to him that he might be going to all this trouble for nothing. Taggert was probably hoofing it down the road right now, ten miles away, and halfway to San Manuel. But Slater never took chances when he didn't have to.

He did not head due east, into the rising sun,

but rather tacked northeast, then southeast, changing directions often. It was foolish to put the sun in your eyes when watching for ambush.

Late in the morning, he spotted dust rising from the flat, over where the road was. Too far to make out the source of the dust, he assumed it to be Amanda Woodbine and her cavalry escort. Slater was confident that they were in no danger of Apache bushwhacking. Of course, there were no ironclad guarantees when you were dealing with a clever bastard like Chacon.

Those Tenth Cavalry yellow-legs were veterans. If worse came to worst, Slater was sure they would do what had to be done—what he would do, if ambushed and overrun. Put a bullet between the woman's eyes.

Slater watched the dust for a spell, then moved on.

Close to sundown, he reached San Manuel.

The town didn't amount to much: a sorry cluster of adobe structures around a square, backed up against a steep range of craggy mountains, and smack in the middle of the San Pedro Valley. Above the town, on a slope of scrub cedar, stood a church. Between the slope and the town was the wide, rocky Cabrito Wash, which remained bone-dry most of the year. Occasionally a flash flood would come roaring down out of the mountains, sometimes taking part of San Manuel with it.

The town's trademark was the turkey buzzards that were often perched in the scrawny cottonwoods along the road on the western outskirts. They seemed to be waiting for the town to die.

This evening, though, San Manuel looked more lively than Slater had ever seen it.

Entering the square in the gray twilight, he noticed quite a few horses hitched to the tie-rails. Yellow light blazed from the doors and windows of the town's only cantina. Someone was strumming a guitar, and men were shouting and laughing. Passing by, Slater took a quick glance through a window, and saw a dark-haired senorita performing the fandango on a tabletop, tossing a brightly-hued skirt to reveal long legs.

The cantina was located on a corner, where the street emptied into the square. A man stepped out of the shadows at the corner and into Slater's path.

By habit, Slater rode with the reins in his left hand. The right, resting on his thigh, moved to the butt of the holstered Schofield .45, thumb on hammer, finger on the trigger. He did not waste time drawing the revolver, merely twisting the holster to line up the shot.

He checked the claybank. Even in the gloom of the gathering night, his eyes were as keen as a mountain cat's. He made an identification prior to the hombre stepping into the throw of light from the window of the cantina.

Seeing Slater's hand on the Schofield, the man tried to edge around to the claybank's offside. Slater would have none of that; he worked the rein leather just so, and the responsive horse pivoted to thwart the man's sidestep.

Slater saw the flash of teeth as big and blunt as headstones when the man grinned at him.

"Slater, I wondered when you'd show up."

"Been expectin' me, Gault?"

Despite Slater's unfriendly tone of voice, Ben Gault kept that counterfeit grin going strong. He was tall and barrel-chested, wearing desert moccasins and grimy buckskins. His spade beard was stained yellow by tobacco juice, and his hair, long and unkempt, fell to his shoulders. He carried a Colt Double Action Army .45 and a long skinning knife in his belt. His weapon of preference, though, was the bullwhacker's whip coiled and carried over his shoulder. With a hickory handle three feet long, the whip was twenty feet of braided-rawhide pain and death in the hands of an expert like Ben Gault. It was said that Gault had skinned a man alive up in Mogollon with that whip.

"Hell yes, I been expecting you, hoss. You're 'bout the only damned bounty man in the Territory what ain't here."

Slater warily searched the shadows beyond Gault.

"Your brothers in town?"

"Why, sure. Joe and Ted and me, we're a team. They're inside suckin' up nose-paint and watchin' that cute little bean'eater gal strut her stuff. C'mon in and join the hoedown, Slater. I'll buy you some snakehead."

"I'll pass." Slater steered clear of other bounty hunters, as would any man with a murder charge hanging over him. Beyond that, he harbored a strong dislike for the Gault brothers. They had started out as muleskinners, and turned to scalp-hunting. The Mexican government still paid good money for Apache scalps. Rumor had it that the Gaults weren't too particular about whose hair they lifted. The scalps of Navajo or Yaqui—not to mention Mexican women—could hardly be distinguished from Apache scalps.

Ben Gault's grin was resembling a snarl as he stepped closer and latched onto the claybank's bridle before Slater could get the horse moving. The claybank snorted and jerked its head back. Slater cocked the Schofield's hammer.

"Watch your manners, Gault."

Gault dispensed with all pretense. His gravelly voice was harsh, like a handful of pebbles ground together.

"You aim to try and collect the bounty on Chacon, Slater?"

"Let go my horse," muttered Slater.

Gault swayed precariously on the brink of disaster for a moment. Reason prevailed, though, as he realized that Slater had the drop on him. Even as he saw the murder fade from Gault's eyes, Slater reckoned that one day, sooner or later, he and Ben Gault were going to have it out.

Letting go of the bridle, Gault stepped back.

"I hope you ain't," he said. "'Cause me and my brothers plan to spend that five thousand dollars the governor's offerin'. We'd be almighty riled, was you to try and keep us from it."

Making no reply, Slater urged the claybank on into the square. He kept his hand on the Schofield and his ears tuned to the slightest hostile sound from behind.

Gault made no move. Just stood there in the road and hatefully watched Slater ride on.

Another man slipped around the corner of the cantina and joined the buckskin-clad scalphunter. He wore a serape to conceal the four guns he carried, two in cross-draw holsters on his lean shanks, and two more in shoulder harnesses. His hat hung by its chinstrap down his back. He looked somewhat like a Mexican *pistolero*, but was in fact Gault's brother, Joe. Joe Gault, quick-draw artist, was more than a match for any gunhawk on either side of the Bloody Border.

"I coulda shot him straight to hell, Ben," said Joe in his whispery voice.

"He knew you was there all along."

"The hell you say."

"Don't underestimate Sam Slater," warned Ben.

Joe Gault snorted. "You think he's gonna go after Chacon?"

"I dunno. He's the one man who could give us a run for our money, if he does. Hell, he's lived with those stinkin' Cherry Cows. He's half-'Pache."

"So what are we gonna do?"

Ben Gault was tugging at his beard, frowning in thought.

"I reckon we got two choices. Either we talk him into joining us, or we have to kill him."

"I say kill him now and be done with it."

Joe took a half-step before his older brother lashed out and gathered up a handful of serape to stop him.

"Not here. Not now. I'll say when the time comes. We'll do the deed together. We'll only get one chance. With a man like Slater, you don't get a second."

CHAPTER 7

THE SAN MANUEL *JUZGADO* WAS ON THE other side of the square from the cantina. Sheriff Heck Digby was sitting in a rocking chair beneath the picket overhang fronting the adobe building. The door of the jail was open. Within, a lamp burned brightly, but Digby was careful to sit in deep shadow. The chair creaked complaint as the badge-toter rocked slowly. A half-empty bottle of mescal stood on the hardpack beside the chair. A sawed-off Davenport shotgun lay across the lawman's lap.

As Slater checked the claybank in front of the jail, Digby said, "Wondered when you'd show."

The bounty man stepped out of the saddle.

Digby carried on. "Governor's in town. Set himself up in the bank. Says he'll pay five thousand simoleons to the man what brings Chacon's head to him in a sack. Says he'll stay put 'til it's done."

"I heard."

Taking the wanted poster from under his shirt, Slater unfolded it, and gave it to Digby. The sheriff tilted the sweat-stained paper so that the light slanting out through the doorway fell upon the crudely-rendered likeness of Bitteroot Carson.

"This is a stage company reward, Slater. Take the stiff on down the street. I got enough trouble on my hands with this damned hardcase convention."

Slater walked back to the dun mare. Using his clasp knife, he cut the rope that lashed the dead longrider to the saddle, and transferred the corpse to his shoulder. Carrying this gruesome load over to Digby, he let it drop at the lawdog's feet. One of Carson's arms flopped onto Digby's leg, and Digby kicked it away.

"Jesus H. Christ," muttered the sheriff, disgusted. "He's starting to ripen. Get him out of my air, Slater. You deaf? I told you. . . ."

"I heard you. Law says all I got to do is deliver the goods to a duly-constituted peace officer. Hard to believe, but that means you, Digby."

"Whadya mean by that crack?" growled Digby.

Slater gave the sheriff a long, hard look. Digby didn't look like much. A pot-bellied, hairy specimen with the pockmarked face and inflamed eyes of a man who suffered from a chronic recurrence of syphilis. He wore dirty, suspendered trousers, and the four-pointed star was pinned to the top half of his soiled pink under-riggings. The straw sombrero on his head looked like someone had hacked on it for an hour with a machete. To Slater's sensitive nose, he smelled worse than Carson's souring carcass.

The bounty man knew, though, that in Digby's case, appearances were indeed deceiving. San Manuel's shotgun-toting law was a dangerous, poor-dispositioned man, as much a hardcase as the hombres raising hell in the cantina across the way. Both barrels in the back—that was Digby's preferred way of dispensing justice in his bailiwick. He was not the kind of man who would give anyone a fair break, if he could help it.

"I mean," replied Slater, "that there's the stiff. Now where's the money?"

"I'll have to find Billings, the express agent, and get him down here to verify. If he ain't got the money in his safe, we'll have to wait 'til mornin', when the bank opens."

Slater grimaced. This was a development he had failed to foresee. Now it appeared that he had spent all day catfooting through the hills, avoiding an ambush that might never have been, and as a result reached San Manuel too late for quick pay-off. The prospect of staying overnight in a townful of manhunters was an unattractive one.

"By the way," continued Digby, "I seem to re-call this no-account Carson held up a stage couple weeks back. Made off with over a thousand dol-lars. You find that loot on him, Slater?"

Digby's tone was sarcastic and suspicious. Slater didn't care for what the lawdog was imply-ing, but he was used to it. Folks just naturally tended to suspect bounty hunters of keeping the ill-gotten gains of the outlaws they tracked down. Some did. Slater didn't. The only money he wanted was the money he had coming to him.

"He had $11.42 on him the day he met his Maker," replied Slater coldly. "And it's still on him."

"Uh-huh." Digby let skepticism drip from that grunted comment.

Slater got provoked. Digby was trying to nettle him out of pure orneriness—and succeeding. Chances were that Bitteroot hadn't garnered any-where close to a thousand out of his last holdup. Individuals and businesses who transferred cash and valuables in a stage company strongbox in-variably claimed greater losses than actually suf-fered, in order to cover past or future graft, or as a means by which larger claims could be made against the carrier. Digby knew this as well as Slater did.

"You're full of horseshit, Digby," said Slater.

Digby tightened his grip on the 10-gauge scattergun. Slater did not react to this menacing move, and the badgetoter stopped short of actually aiming the sawed-off at the bounty hunter. Slater's faint smile was mocking. Digby was a backshooter. This was macho bluff.

"I'll be back in an hour for the reward," said Slater.

He turned his back on Digby, a contemptuous act, gathered up the reins of the ground-hitched claybank, and began to walk both horses away from the San Manuel hoosegow. The dun mare was still on a lead rope dallied to Slater's saddlehorn.

"Slater!"

Slater turned, casual. He had been listening for the Davenport's hammers being cocked, and hadn't heard the sound. Digby wanted to see him jump, that was all. But Slater wasn't the nervous sort.

"I reckon that mare was Carson's. The saddle and long-rifle, too. Where you goin' with it?"

"Where do you think?"

"Stage company may want to confiscate anything of value Carson had on him. Cut their losses."

"They'd better find another way of doing that."

"You goin' after that sonuvabitch Chacon?"

"You taking a poll?"

The sheriff hefted the bottle of mescal and took a couple of long swallows. He drank the potent cactus juice like it was water, and wiped his mouth with a sleeve.

"Just wonderin'. Thought I might even take a shot at that five thousand myself."

"Forget that," advised Slater. "Chacon won't let you sneak up behind him."

Digby's expression darkened. "I'll overlook that remark."

"Somehow I knew you would," replied Slater and moved on.

CHAPTER 8

HIS FIRST STOP WAS THE LIVERY AT THE north end of San Manuel, owned and operated by a little old Mexican with seven sons, every one of whom was strong enough to carry a horse on his back. Some wondered how such huge offspring could have come from the loins of such a small man.

The livery yard was encircled by a crumbling adobe wall. The stables were adobe, waist-high, and completed with cedar and mesquite pickets. Tonight there were quite a few horses boarded within. Slater noted that four carried the vent brands of the Tenth Cavalry. These, then, were the mounts of Amanda Woodbine's cavalry escort. So the young woman had made it to safety.

The old Mexican was happy to see Slater. He was always in the market for cut-rate horseflesh. They settled down to haggling, sharing a bottle of tequila. Slater felt a hundred percent better with a bellyful of liquid fire. The Mexican offered him the worm, but Slater graciously declined.

One of the old man's sons was hard at work at the forge. The clang of iron and the hiss of the bellows filled the night. A second son took charge of Slater's claybank, leading the horse to a stall. The claybank was in good hands. It would be grained and watered and curried. Another son squatted off a ways and just watched the business proceedings. Nobody in his right mind gave the old man a hard time with a bodyguard of those dimensions so near at hand.

The Mexican was a skinflint. It took a spell, but Slater finally got the price for the dun mare up to fifty dollars. He threw in the saddle gratis. The old man wanted the Winchester repeater that had belonged to the Apache lookout, but Slater refused to include such a fine weapon in the deal. Eventually the old Mexican consented to paying five dollars for the suspect Colt sidehammer once owned by Bitteroot Carson, and free board for the claybank. Slater reckoned that was the level best he could hope to get for an antique like the sidehammer.

His next stop was the store run by the Dutchman named Holzer. The shebang was locked up tighter than a fat lady's stocking. Slater knew that the shopkeeper lived in a small room at the rear of the adobe house, and kept pounding on the door until he got a response. It wasn't exactly the response he'd expected. The gaunt, owlish emigrant with the thick spectacles opened the door and stuck an old Colt Dragoon in Slater's face.

"Vot you vant?"

"Hike those see-betters higher on your nose, Doc."

Holzer did just that. Recognizing Slater, he lowered the pistol. His expression altered from apprehensive to apologetic.

"Sam Slater! *Mein Gott*, I am sorry. Come in, come in."

Slater stepped inside. Holzer bolted the door and fired up a kerosene lamp. The bounty hunter laid the Winchester and Bitteroot Carson's shell-belt and sixgun on the dry-goods counter. He kept his own Spencer carbine shoulder-racked, and threw a look around the shebang. Like most frontier general stores, Holzer's was separated with foodstuffs on one side and dry goods on the other. Stocked shelves rose to the ceiling on either side. A person could find just about anything at

Holzer's, from linen to linament, airtights to ammo.

"What's wrong, Doc?"

Holzer had become San Manuel's resident sawbones by default. He didn't have any formal training in medicine, but he knew a thing or two about practical field application. He could treat colic or remove a bullet, depending on the need. Those who doubted the efficacy of the herb potions and bloodletting of the half-breed, hundred-year-old *curandero* on the other side of town came to the Dutchman.

Holzer scowled. "I tell you vot, Sam. Zis town is full of bad men. All of a sudden, zey swoop down like vultures."

"Least you're safe from Apaches," smiled Slater.

Holzer snorted. "Six of one, half-dozen of the odder, you ask me. So Sam, vot haf ve here? You brought anodder one to justice?"

"You could say that. How much can I get for this?"

"A fine rifle. You should keep it for yourself, unt sell me dat one you haf now."

"Nope. This .56 has never let me down. I'll stick with it."

"But vit zis Winchester, you can use the same ammunition."

"Sorry, Doc. I'll will the .56 to you. You can have it when I'm no longer above snakes."

"Vell, I may not haf to wait long, considering der business you are in." Holzer checked the action of the Winchester. Slater snatched the ejected shell out of the air and laid it on the counter. The store-owner then examined the Colt Civilian with the hand and eye of a man who knew his way around firearms.

"I vill give twenty dollars for der rifle, Sam. Unt twelve more for der rest."

Slater nodded. As Holzer got the money from the cashbox under the counter, he said, "The vultures didn't take long to gather."

"Ven his daughter vas taken, der governor sent telegrams all over the territory. I am told every newspaper printed der reward notice. For zat kind of money, men vould ride zare horses into der ground, no?"

"I reckon. Not much chance I'd find a bunk at Mama Garcia's is there?"

Holzer shook his head emphatically. "But you can stay here, Sam. Unt *wilkommen*." He slapped the counter-top with the palm of his hand. "Sleep right here, and be comfortable. No charge."

Slater smiled. He didn't consider himself to be any better than the men Doc Holzer was afraid of, but if the Dutchman trusted him, who was he to argue with the arrangement? In exchange for the boarding, he would gladly shoot to hell and gone any hombre who thought to mess with Doc or the store.

"It's a deal," he said, and shook the storekeeper's bony hand to seal the bargain.

Gathering up his thirty-two dollars, he turned for the door.

"Vere you goink, Sam?"

"Won't be long, Doc. Got some more dinero to collect."

"You vill be goink after the Apaches?"

"Not this child," replied Slater with absolute conviction. "Last time I saw them, they were heading west. I'll go the other direction come sunrise."

"Vy? You are not afraid of zem." It was a statement; Holzer was of the opinion that Sam Slater was afraid of nothing and nobody.

"I don't hunt Apaches." Unlocking the door, Slater stepped out into moonshadow. "Be easy on the trigger, Doc. I'll be back plenty pronto."

Slater bent his steps toward the center of town. Crossing the square, he could tell that the action was still going strong in the cantina across the way. Normally, he patronized the place when in San Manuel. Considering the clientele that was in there now, though, he intended to steer well clear.

Two dark shapes stumbled out of a doorway blazing with light. Slater stopped. He saw a muzzle-flash, and the gunshot bent him into a crouch, the Spencer swept down to hip level. The report was followed by drunken laughter. Another muzzle-flash, above the men, another booming crack. They were shooting at the stars, realized Slater. Raising a little hell. Slater expected to see Digby slinking across the square, on the hunt for a chance to bushwhack, but didn't. The men stumbled into the shadows, moving away from the square and Slater. The bounty hunter pressed on.

Drawing near the jail, he noticed that the rocking chair was empty, the door closed. Carson's body had been removed.

Slater didn't think twice about that. He stepped, bold as brass, through the door into the front office of the jail.

And froze at the feel of a gunbarrel pressed against the back of his skull, by someone who had waited behind the door.

Digby was sitting behind his desk, grinning at Slater over a smoldering cheroot. The sawed-off shotgun lay in front of him on the clutter of old newspapers and wanted posters that blanketed the desktop.

"Don't move, Slater," warned the man behind the bounty hunter. "You do, I'll splatter your brains all over that there wall."

Slater recognized the voice, and felt his guts twist.

Taggert.

"Yeah," said Digby, "and that would piss me off no end. This place is messy enough, as is."

"Violence won't be necessary, gentlemen."

This assurance came from a third man, who emerged, stooping, through the low-slung doorway to the cellblock.

He was a trim, older man in a handsome brown broadcloth suit. His boots were polished bench-made Middletons. His hat was a homburg with a brown satin band. He sported a cane with a staghorn ferrule. Gray-streaked sideburns met the tips of a luxuriant moustache. Slater looked past the pleasant smile and saw the sharp features of a shrewd and determined individual.

"Who the hell are you?" rasped Slater, angry at himself for waltzing straight into an ambush.

"John Clay Woodbine, Mr. Slater. Governor of this great territory."

"No shit."

Woodbine stepped closer. "Mr. Taggert, I'll thank you to shut the door."

Taggert kicked the door closed. He didn't ease off on the gun jammed against Slater's head.

"Don't get too close, Governor," advised Taggert. "This one's mean as a rabid dog."

"Oh, I believe Mr. Slater will act like a reasonable man."

Slater's grin was about as reasonable as the snarl of a wolf.

"You dead sure about that, Governor?" he asked.

CHAPTER 9

"DROP THE CARBINE," SAID TAGGERT. "THEN the sidegun, belt and all."

Slater tossed the Spencer across the room. "Here, Digby, Fetch."

The sheriff wasn't expecting that. He tried to catch the .56/50, but missed. The Spencer struck his arm and fell onto the desk, overturning a bottle of mescal. What little liquor was left in the bottle splattered the paper clutter. The cheroot fell out of Digby's mouth and into his lap. The badge-toter almost toppled out of his chair trying to avoid being burned in the worst possible place.

Taggert pressed harder with the gun, forcing Slater's head forward.

"You're a tick's hair from being one dead sonuvabitch," he said through gritted teeth. "Now *drop* the gunbelt. Don't go throwin' the damned thing around."

Slater used his left hand to unfasten the belt buckle. He let the shellbelt and Schofield drop. Taggert kicked them away.

Digby looked at the spilled mescal, crestfallen, then glowered at Slater. Rising, he punted the chair out of his way, stooped to retrieve the cheroot, grunting heavily.

"Careful, Sheriff," said Slater, his tone insulting. "Don't hurt yourself. I swear, you sound like a woman in labor. With that belly you got, you sorta look like one, come to think of it."

The lawdog straightened, gnashing violently on the cheroot clenched in his teeth. He was red in the face, both from exertion and embarrassment. Grabbing the scattergun, he stalked around the desk, moving ominously towards Slater.

"Take it easy, Sheriff," said Governor Woodbine. It was more a command than a suggestion. "He's only trying to rile you."

"He done a bang-up job," growled Digby. He got right up into Slater's face. "You're a real hardcase, ain't you?" he sneered.

Slater did not flinch from the cheroot's biting smoke or the foul stench of Digby's breath.

"Here's your chance," he said, contemptuous. "I'm unarmed."

Digby spat in his face.

"That's what I think of you and your kind."

Slater still didn't move. Yellow spittle ran down his cheek.

Digby started turning away, looking satisfied. But Slater knew that the sheriff wasn't finished. Digby was just trying to lure him off his guard.

Spinning, the lawman slammed the sawed-off Davenport into Slater's gut. Slater was braced and ready, but he acted like the blow hurt him badly. He jackknifed forward and fell.

Digby started laughing. The laughter turned into a screech as Slater drove his fist up between the sheriff's legs. Digby dropped the greener and clutched his private parts, whirling away.

As Taggert brought his handgun down to aim at Slater, the bounty man lunged upright, knocking Taggert's gunarm aside and ramming a fist into the man's jaw. The gun went off, the bullet punching into the ceiling. Slater drove Taggert into the wall with the full weight of his body. He jabbed Taggert in the sternum. Taggert doubled over. Slater brought his knee up into the man's face. Blood sprayed out of Taggert's nose and mouth as his knees turned to rubber and he pitched forward.

Slater let him go, wrenching the gun out of the man's grasp, and spun to the sound of hammers being cocked.

Governor Woodbine had Digby's scattergun aimed at the bounty hunter.

Calm and unruffled in this whirlwind of violence, Woodbine said, "Be so kind as to drop that pistol, Mr. Slater. I don't want to have to kill you. But I will, if you force the issue. I've killed men before. I won't hesitate."

With a bleak half-smile, Slater tossed Taggert's gun away. Woodbine was in deadly earnest.

Digby was over by the desk, on his knees and making terrible guttural noises as he dry-heaved. Taggert was groveling on the floor between Slater and the governor. Woodbine looked at this, Slater's five-second handiwork, with a clinical eye.

"You're a dangerous man." He sounded downright pleased with this discovery. "Few men who found themselves under the gun would dare to do what you just did."

"I've got nothing to lose."

"Bear that in mind, as you listen to my proposition."

"Proposition?"

Taggert was trying to get up. Blood drooled from his cut lip. He spat out a couple of dislodged teeth. On hands and knees, he turned his head slowly. He saw Slater standing over him, and the gun Slater had just thrown down. He lunged clumsily for the gun. Slater took one long stride and kicked it out from under his groping hand.

"Be still, Taggert," said Woodbine sharply. "I don't want him dead."

"I do," muttered Taggert. "So go to hell, Governor."

"I'll send you instead, sir, if you persist."

Taggert heard something that worried him in Woodbine's quietly resolute voice. He rolled over into a sitting position, looked at the twin barrels of the Davenport aimed at a spot between him and Slater, then glowered furiously at Digby.

"Digby, you dunderplated idiot. We shoulda killed this bastard Slater ourselves. But no, you had to go spill the whole goddamn can of beans to the governor here."

The San Manuel lawman was in no condition to reply.

"The sheriff did the right thing, Mr. Taggert," said Woodbine. "Though for the wrong reasons." The governor turned his attention back to Slater. "I suppose you'd like to know what's going on here."

Slater shrugged. "You're gonna tell me anyway."

"Yes. Yes, I am. Mr. Taggert came to Sheriff Digby and claimed that you were a wanted man,

Mr. Slater. Wanted for murder, up Montana way. Isn't that right, Mr. Taggert?"

"Yeah," grumbled Taggert, put out by this unexpected turn of events. "I was a station agent for the Overland up there. I had me a vested interest in keepin' tabs on all the local longriders." He cast a jaundiced eye upon Slater. "I'd know that face anywheres. Seen it many a time on wanted posters up north. Cain't hardly mistake it, with that scar."

"Mr. Taggert came to the sheriff for help," Woodbine told Slater. "I don't think he wanted to try you on alone."

"That ain't straight!" protested Taggert. "I just wanted to be sure there was still a price on his head. Figured Heck could find out."

"Come now," admonished Woodbine. "You could have sent a wire yourself to determine as much. Admit it, Mr. Taggert. You were willing to share the reward with Sheriff Digby in exchange for help in collecting it. And you knew that the sheriff would assist you, if the price were right."

Taggert resentfully refused to admit any such thing.

"The sheriff then came to me," Woodbine said, again addressing Slater. "Unbeknownst to Mr. Taggert. I believe your reputation gave him second thoughts. He asked me to send for a couple of territorial marshals to assist him. As territorial marshals are not themselves permitted to collect reward money, Sheriff Digby would still get his bounty. Whether he intended to share the proceeds with Mr. Taggert is a matter of conjecture. And, at this point, moot."

"You've got the wrong man," said Slater flatly. "I've never been to Montana."

Taggert snorted.

Woodbine smiled. "I didn't expect you to admit it."

"You're making a mistake."

"Well, I could have you locked up in this jail until such time as I received confirmation from Montana. That could take quite a long time. Or, you could accept my proposition, and live in this territory—safe from men like Taggert—for as long as I am governor."

"What do I have to do?"

Some of the polish came off Woodbine then.

"Hunt down and kill that bastard Apache renegade, Chacon."

CHAPTER 10

"HE'S NOT A BASTARD," SAID SLATER. "I KNEW both his father and his mother."

"That's precisely my point. You know the Apache better than any white man, save, perhaps, Al Seiber or Tom Horn. You lived with them. Sheriff Digby tells me that your adoptive father was Chacon's father, as well."

"You've got fifteen, twenty men out there. Ready, willing and able to hunt down Chacon and his renegades. Well, maybe not able, but ready and willing. All they're waiting on is word from you personally that this talk about five thousand dollars in reward money isn't just so much corral dust."

"And I will make a public announcement to-morrow morning. I will place the money in a special account at the San Manuel Bank. But my instincts tell me that you have a better chance than all of them put together. If you have lived with the Apache then you must think like them, hunt like them. Kill like them."

"Your army has Apache scouts."

"The army," scoffed Woodbine. "When was the last time the army managed to catch and defeat an Apache raiding party?"

Slater grimaced. Woodbine had him over a barrel. The past was one thing a man could never completely escape.

"Say I agree, Governor. Say I then ride out of here and just keep on riding?"

"Then I will personally pay another five thousand dollars for your head. I'll hire men to track you to the ends of the earth. But I still believe that you are a reasonable man. And that my offer is too good to refuse."

"All this, just because of what happened to your daughter?"

Cold fury, barely contained, rippled over Woodbine's distinguished features.

"You speak of it in a very cavalier manner, Mr. Slater. I don't appreciate that. Do you know what they did to her?"

"Sure, I know. I'm the one got her away from

the Apaches in the first place, turned her over to the cavalry."

"Captain Mack sent a report back with her escort. He was rather vague with details concerning her rescue at Ghost Springs."

"I asked him to keep me out of it."

"You tell me now because you hope I'll be grateful enough to let you off the hook." Woodbine shook his head adamantly. "I *am* grateful. But I want Chacon dead. Do you understand, Mr. Slater? I won't be satisfied with his recapture. I don't want him back in chains. I want him dead and buried."

"What if I do kill Chacon? How you going to keep these two quiet?" Slater gestured at Taggert and Digby. Both men were still on the floor, recovering slowly.

"Money."

"And if they come after me anyway?"

"Then kill them. I don't think you'd have much trouble with these two. I'll guarantee you full immunity from prosecution in that event."

Taggert, incredulous, stared at Woodbine. The governor had just given Sam Slater permission to punch his ticket, and the sheriff's. That didn't do much to lift Taggert's spirits.

Woodbine went on. "I can see that you don't entirely trust me to fulfill my end of the bargain, Mr. Slater."

"Don't take it personal. I don't trust anybody."

"You're wondering if I'll doublecross you. If I'll clap you in irons after you bring Chacon's head to me. Well, you have my word. I'd make a deal with the devil himself to get Chacon."

"That's what you're doing, Governor," interjected Taggert.

Woodbine ignored the remark. "Slater, if my word isn't good enough for you, then you'll just have to take the chance. I don't see any other alternative open to you."

Slater drew a long breath. "I don't either."

"Then we have an agreement."

"Agreement? Looks more like blackmail from where I'm standing."

"In politics, you learn to do whatever it takes to get the job done."

"If you say so."

"So we have a deal?"

Slater nodded.

"Then you are free to go, Mr. Slater."

"Not yet. I've got five hundred dollars coming for Bitteroot Carson."

"Where are you staying the night?"

"Doc Holzer's."

"I'll have the money to you in an hour."

"I hope so. 'Cause I don't want to have to come back down here to get it."

"No. And I'm confident that Sheriff Digby doesn't want you to, either."

Slater collected his weapons, draping the shellbelt over his shoulder. He was about to depart the jail when Governor Woodbine spoke again.

"Just between us, Mr. Slater. Can you catch him? Can you track Chacon down and kill him?"

"Oh, I can kill him, Governor. If he doesn't snuff my candle first. But I won't have to catch him. He'll come to me." Slater spared Taggert and Digby a final glance and a desolate smile. "See you boys around."

He stepped out into the night.

Outside the jailhouse, Slater paused to study the night. He was feeling at loose ends, and in a poor frame of mind. He was also feeling trapped. He didn't like that feeling one damned bit.

Woodbine was all the way right. There weren't any options open to him. His best bet in this sucker game was to shoot daylight through Chacon and hope that the governor kept his word.

The thought came to him that he probably wouldn't have to worry about the Governor's integrity. Odds were good that he'd be the one with toes permanently curled, not Chacon.

He wasn't going to chase Chacon and his Apache brethren. That would be like digging his own grave. No, his only chance was to lure Chacon into an ambush, on ground of his own choosing. He knew exactly how to accomplish this. He'd worked the scheme out in his mind during today's long ride from Corto Agua. Just a mental exercise, for at the time he'd had no plans to go hunting Chacon. Now, it seemed, his plans were changed. Or, more accurately, had been changed for him.

Strapping on his shellbelt and tying down the holster, Slater started across the moon-bright square, making for the cantina. He needed a good, stiff drink, and by God he was going to have one. To hell with avoiding the congregation of bounty hunters. In a way he was the governor's man now. He had a license to kill from Woodbine himself, and for as long as Woodbine thought him the only man capable of getting Chacon. If one of the manhunters in the cantina gave him any problems he'd put spit in the bastard's eye and lead in his guts.

Like a cornered wolf, Slater was all through running and hiding. Throwing caution to the wind, and thumbing the leather thong off the Schofield's hammer, he stalked, hard-eyed, into San Manuel's one and only "hog ranch."

The woman wasn't dancing anymore. She was sitting in Ben Gault's lap, at the table which the elder Gault shared with his two brothers. The woman whispered something in Ben's ear, and Ben threw his head back and let loose a guffaw that shook the walls. Joe Gault wore a tight smile as he watched Ben and the woman cavort. Slater figured that Joe wanted the woman in his own lap. But he was going to have to settle for the consolation provided by the bottle of Taos Lightning he was fast emptying.

Slater remembered that Joe carried four pistols under the serape. He was prone to boasting that he could kill twenty-four men with the twenty-four bullets in the chambers of those pistols. No question but that Joe Gault was a quick draw with a dead eye.

The youngest brother, Ted, was a thin, pale boy wearing dirty woolen pants, a linsey-woolsey shirt and a battered, old derby pulled low over furtive eyes. Slack in a tipped-back chair, he was bouncing one leg and then the other, and flipping a knife in the air with one hand. He looked as restless and neurotic as ever. Where Ben preferred the bullwhip and Joe the gun, Ted was a blade man at heart. He carried a pair of pearl-handled Bowie knives in sheaths on his hips.

Several men, looking no less rough and dangerous than the brothers Gault, were at another table playing Mexican Sweat, betting both coin and cartridges. A couple more were bellied up to the bar, planks laid across barrels. Slater reckoned that they were all here waiting to hear it from the governor himself that there was indeed a five-thousand-dollar reward for the head of the renegade Chacon. Trying to get Chacon would be a highly risky business, and these men wanted to hear it from the horse's mouth before putting their lives on the line.

They all gave Slater a careful once-over as he angled across to the bar. Slater felt his muscles bunch and his heart quicken. He knew what it felt like to be a wanted man. And he used that knowledge to his advantage. The secret to his success as a bounty hunter was his unique ability to get into the minds of the men he hunted, to put himself in their boots.

No one made a move against him, though. Apparently none of these manhunters could match his appearance to any of the wanted posters with which they were familiar.

A Mexican man was sitting in a corner, strumming a guitar, impassively watching Ben Gault and the woman. He was the senorita's father. She supported the family by dancing and catering to the lusts of the cantina's clientele. If he was bothered by the bold wanderings of Ben Gault's hands, he didn't show it. *We all do what we have to in order to survive,* mused Slater. He figured the man would not intervene unless Gault got violent and damaged the merchandise.

She wasn't the only whore in town, but she *was* the only one working the cantina tonight. Though short on looks, she would never want for business in this country. There weren't enough women in these parts that men could afford to be discriminating. Beggars could not be choosers.

"Whiskey," said Slater, laying the Spencer on the bar. "A bottle of your best."

The barkeep nodded, returned a moment later with the order. Slater held the bottle up and scrutinized its amber contents against the back-light of camphene lamps hooked to the wall. Then he popped the cork and sniffed. Raw red-eye, but as far as he could tell, untainted by tabasco or tobacco juice to mask a watering-down.

He was digging into his pocket for payment when Ben Gault slapped a "dobe dollar" on the bartop.

"This one's on me, amigo," he told the bar-keeper.

The Mexican was reaching for the peso when Slater said, "I ordered it. I'll pay for it."

He placed a U.S. cartwheel on the bar.

Gault said, softly, "That's just downright un-friendly, Slater, refusin' to let a friend buy your ass a lousy drink."

Slater turned. Gault had the woman pinned to his side with one burly arm. Next to him, she looked like a small and fragile doll, especially with all the powder and paint on her face.

"Oh, I'd let a *friend* buy me a drink," smiled Slater, looking for trouble. Frustrated by Woodbine's blackmail, he was in no mood to take guff from anybody. Least of all a Gault.

The barkeep reached for Slater's dollar.

Gault growled, "You must be as deaf as you are ugly, apron. I *said* I was payin' for the bottle."

The barkeeper threw up his hands.

"*Muy bien.* The whiskey, it is on the house."

He started to move discreetly away. A storm was brewing, and all he wanted to do was get out of range of the lightning. These gringos, and their foolish, dangerous pride!

"Hey," said Slater.

With a sigh of resignation, the barkeep came back.

"You gonna take my money?" asked Slater, "or do I give it to your next of kin?"

CHAPTER 11

"*SI*," NODDED THE BARTENDER WEARILY. HE snatched up Slater's dollar and beat a hasty retreat to the other end of the bar.

"Slater," said Gault gruffly, retrieving his own coin, "I want a straight answer from you. Are you goin' after that devil Chacon, or not?"

"You writin' a book?"

Gault exhaled sharply through clenched teeth, making a hissing sound.

"No matter. I know damned well you are. Why else would you hang around this stinking town longer than you have to?"

"It sure ain't the company."

"Ow!" yelped the woman. "Hombre, you are hurting me!"

That startled Gault. He'd been squeezing the breath out of the whore without even realizing it. Now he released her, with a little shove to get her started.

"Get on back to the table."

The woman sullenly left them. Slater took a slug of rotgut. He could feel Gault's eyes boring into him. Gault forced a smile.

"I got a proposition for you, Slater."

"This is my night for propositions."

Gault scowled, trying to figure that remark, then gave up trying.

"The deal is this. My brothers and me, we aim to collect that bounty on Chacon. You can bet your firstborn child we'll do it, too. But we're willin' to cut you in as a full partner. Split that five thousand four ways."

"That's mighty white of you."

"Good business, way I see it. We figure your bein' along will make things that much easier. You know the Apache and his ways, even better than us."

Gault paused, expecting a response. Slater tipped the bottle back again. He acted like he hadn't even heard.

"So what d'you say?"

"Maybe you need me, Gault. But I sure as hell don't need you."

Gault's face darkened with anger. He pulled savagely on his beard.

"Don't get crossways with me, Slater. You'll be two-steppin' to a waltz, for certain."

"See you around, Gault."

Gault stood there a full half-minute, forming in his mind a couple more choice remarks of a threatening or insulting nature, but decided against voicing them, and stalked back to his table.

Scarcely had he reclaimed his chair—and the whore—than four Tenth Cavalry buffalo soldiers entered the cantina.

Slater recognized one as the gristleneck first sergeant whom Captain Mack had put in charge of Amanda Woodbine's escort from Ghost Springs. The other three were troopers. They came to the bar. The sergeant remembered Slater from the stage station, and gave a nod. Slater looked away without returning the friendly acknowledgment.

"Whiskey," said the sergeant.

"Yeah, four bottles," said an eager private.

"*One* bottle, dammit," corrected the sergeant. "We'll share. We's goin' back out into Apacheria, boys, and I want you all cold sober when them *cimarrones* stake you down over an antbed and commence to cuttin' off your *cajones.*"

"Got to say, Sarge, you have a real pretty way of puttin' things."

The barkeep went to fetch a bottle. He was returning to the horse soldiers when the Bowie knife passed right in front of his eyes. The knife thunked into the adobe wall behind the bar. The barkeep made a sound that was half-gasp, half-yell. He jumped back, tripped over his own feet, and fell heavily. The bottle hit the hardpack but did not shatter, rolling instead between the barrels supporting the bar and coming to rest against Slater's left foot.

The guitar-player wasn't playing anymore. Everybody got quiet in a hurry. Except for the Gaults. Ben's deep chuckle sounded like a long roll of distant thunder. Ted was laughing like a hyena. Joe simply smiled.

The bartender got to his feet, his dark face utterly impassive. Ted was suddenly at the bar, six feet to Slater's left. The youngest Gault gathered up a handful of the Mexican's white shirt and yanked the man's face close to his.

"Gimme back my knife, Pancho."

"Si, senor."

Ted let him go with a rough push. The barkeep pulled the knife from the wall. He made the mistake of handing the weapon to Ted hilt-first. His hands were trembling. Grinning, Ted took the Bowie knife and savagely slashed sideways. The barkeeper fell backwards, blood spurting from his fingers where the razor-sharp blade had cut to the bone. He did not cry out.

"You oughta be more careful," crowed Ted.

Out of an eye-corner, Slater saw one of the troopers move. The sergeant's arm came up like a gate pole to stop the private's forward progress.

Wiping the bloodied blade on his pants leg, Ted said, "Beaneater, you oughta thank me. I done kept you from makin' one almighty big mistake. Why, do you realize that you was about to serve niggers in this here establishment? Now, we just don't do that sort of thing 'round these parts, hoss."

The barkeep looked up slowly, his eyes as blank as a diamondback rattler's.

Bending, Slater picked up the bottle. He set it on the bar. Ted Gault looked over at him. His smile was lopsided, his glittering eyes hooded.

Slater slid the bottle to his right, down the planking of the bar. The sergeant caught it.

"What the hell d'you think you're doing?" challenged Ted, his voice shrill, his tone incredulous.

"Back off, Ted," barked Ben Gault from the table. He wasn't laughing any longer.

But Ted seemed not to hear his oldest brother's command.

"You lousy nigger-lover," he sneered, turning to brace Slater, Bowie knife in hand.

"Sergeant!" groaned one of the troopers, pleading for permission to light into Ted Gault.

The sergeant spun to face his men. "Atten-*shun!*" he snapped, each syllable cracking like a rifle shot.

The three troopers snapped to.

Ted Gault found this to be a highly amusing spectacle.

"Well, will you look at that," he jeered. "Ain't that somethin' special? They almost look like real soldier-boys. But they ain't too keen on fightin', are they?"

"You haven't seen the Tenth in action," remarked Slater. "Or you wouldn't say that."

Ted's features turned ugly. "I've had about enough of you, Slater."

He took two threatening steps towards Slater.

"Ted, you fool. . . ." growled Ben Gault.

Slater saw the lamplight flash off the blade of the Bowie knife. Quicker than the eye, he grabbed his bottle of whiskey by the neck and spun. His right arm knocked Ted's knife-hand aside and the left brought the bottle around full-swing to smash the youngest Gault's face. The bottle shattered. Ted bounced off the bar, keeled sideways. He rolled over, uttering short ragged grunts, got his knees up under him, then flopped onto his side. His hands covered his face. Blood trickled through the clawing fingers.

The guttural wail he let go then sent a cold chill down Slater's spine.

"*Madre de Dios*," muttered the guitar-player, thoroughly shaken by the sound.

"Son of a bitch," said Joe, without rancor, without inflection of any kind.

He came out of his chair in a fast crouching spin. The chair fell over.

In that split-second it occurred to Slater that Joe Gault meant to draw down on him.

And he didn't have a chance in hell of beating the gunslinger.

With a roar like that of a wounded grizzly, Ben Gault rose up, spilling the shrieking whore out of his lap, and shoving the table forward as hard as he could. The edge of the table caught Joe in the back of the legs. He pitched forward, in the process of whipping the pistols out of the cross-draw holsters on his hips. He hit the hardpack floor, rolled, and came up in a fighting stance, hands full of iron.

This gave Slater the precious extra second he needed to draw his own gun.

"No!" bellowed Ben Gault, stepping into the line of fire. "No shooting!" He speared Slater with a fierce glower, then his brother.

"Ben, look what he done to Ted," said Joe. Despite the lethal tension of the moment, his tone was calm, almost conversational.

"The little runt brought it on hisself," snapped

Ben crossly, looking down at Ted with complete disgust.

"You can't let him get away with. . . ."

"Don't be tellin' me what I can or cain't do," roared Ben ominously. "Slater could've killed him, but didn't. I'd say he was luckier than he has a right to be. Now put those hoglegs away, by damn, 'fore I knock your teeth out."

Showing no emotion, Joe deftly rolled the pistols back into the holsters.

At first, Slater was puzzled. Ben Gault was not one to shy away from violence, or espouse the notion of fair play. Taking a quick look to one side, Slater saw what had motivated the elder Gault to intervene.

All four of the buffalo soldiers had their service revolvers in hand.

And Sheriff Heck Digby stood in the doorway, the Davenport scattergun aimed at the Gault brothers.

CHAPTER 12

BEN GAULT WAS VICIOUS, AMORAL, AND A strong believer in vengeance. But he wasn't stupid.

With that in mind, Slater holstered the Schofield and picked up the Spencer. He turned towards the door. As he passed the buffalo soldiers the sergeant said, "Hey, you."

Slater stopped.

"We don't need nobody fightin' our fights," said the three-striper.

Slater's face might have been carved from granite, for all the emotion it displayed.

The sergeant's grim demeanor eased into a smile.

"But thanks, all the same."

Slater moved on. At the doorway, he started past Digby without sparing the badge-toter a glance.

"I ain't forgettin' what you done to me, Slater," muttered Digby, keeping his eyes—and the barrels of the greener—on the Gaults.

"Then why are you trying to save my bacon, Sheriff?"

"You know why. The governor'd have my ass were anything to happen to you in San Manuel. But there'll come a time and a place, mister. You can bank on that."

"Thanks. You've given me something to look forward to."

He stepped on into the night.

On his way back to Doc Holzer's, it occurred to him that he would have been better off killing Ted Gault. After what he'd done, he would certainly be obliged to sooner or later. Ted would never let something like this lie. None of the Gaults would. Hurt and humiliate one Gault, and you did it to them all.

There was another reason to look out for the Gault brothers. They were dead set on collecting the reward for Chacon, and they weren't about to let him muddy their water on that score. That was all well and good. When the time came, he'd rid the world of the Gaults and consider it a day well spent.

Killing didn't bother him. Life wasn't sacred; it was dirty and short and bitter, filled with pain and hardship. He didn't much mind risking his or taking others. Still, he had to draw the line somewhere. He would kill for bounty, or in self-defense. But not in a dispute over whether a passel of horse soldiers got a bottle of nose-paint or not. If and when Ted Gault came after him, then he would finish the job up right. Then it would be personal. Meanwhile, he could take satisfaction in knowing that the younger Gault was in for a heap of suffering. That improved Slater's mood by a long sight.

When Holzer opened the door of the shebang, Slater knew immediately that something was very wrong.

He could read that much in the Dutchman's anxious eyes. And his keen sense of smell detected the faint aroma of a burning cigarette coming from inside the store.

Holzer didn't smoke.

"Sam, vy do you just stand there? Come in, by golly."

Slater wasn't paying Holzer any attention. He was peering past the old shopkeeper. The store was dark. A lamp was burning in the back room, its light slipping past the edges of the curtain which draped the connecting doorway.

The curtains moved.

Holzer gasped as Slater's hand lashed out and gathered up the front of his shirt. Slater yanked the shopkeeper off his feet and out of the store. The bounty hunter moved sideways, putting his back to the outer wall, and drawing the merchant past him and out of the line of fire. He carried the Spencer in the other hand; thumbed back the hammer.

"Sam!" wheezed Doc, frantic. "For der love of Gott, don't shoot!"

"What?"

"Yes, Mr. Slater. He doesn't want you to shoot me."

The voice belonged to a woman, and it issued from the dark interior of the general store.

"What the hell is going on?" snapped Slater, giving Holzer a hard shake just to assert that he expected an answer, and fast.

"Der governor's dotter, Sam. She has come to see you."

Slater let go of Holzer and stepped into the doorway, the Spencer leveled.

He could see a figure—definitely the figure of a woman. Beyond her the curtains were now slightly parted, and lamplight came through to glimmer off golden hair.

"You should have killed me before," she said.

"Do you want to now? I don't care. Go ahead. You'd be doing me a favor."

Slater lowered the carbine.

"Why are you here?"

"I've got a proposition for you."

Slater laughed.

"Is that funny?" she asked, briskly. "Perhaps you're thinking that a lady of proper breeding would not dare use that term. Well, I'm not exactly a proper young lady. Maybe I was, once. Not any longer. *They've* seen to that."

"They?"

"You know who I mean," she said in a fierce whisper.

"I've got all the business I can handle right now."

"You'd be well-advised to hear me out."

"Doc, get in here and shut the door."

The Dutchman stepped inside, his movements tentative.

"Mr. Holzer," said Amanda Woodbine, "I would prefer to speak to Mr. Slater privately."

Holzer looked all too ready to depart for places unknown, but he glanced at Slater for permission before moving an inch. Slater nodded curtly.

"I vill vait outside."

He went out, closing the door behind him.

"Your father know you're here?"

"Certainly. I knew he was arranging to send you a sum of money. A reward for an outlaw you brought in. I convinced him to let me come along. I told him that I wanted to thank you personally for saving my life."

"And he let you? This time of night, in a town crawling with rough customers?"

"Oh, I'm perfectly safe." She turned her head slightly. "You may come out now, Mr. Blane."

The curtains parted. He was a big man, with shoulders as wide as a doubletree. The brim of his low-crowned hat was down-turned. He wore a slicker, and his spurs rang against the floor planking.

Slater again brought the carbine up. This was purely reflex. He couldn't make anything out except the shape of the man in the slicker, and the orange glowing tip of a roll-your-own a few inches below the hat brim.

"I'd be obliged if you'd point that somewhere else." It was a deep, rumbling voice, as lethally calm as the eye of a hurricane.

"It's all right," Amanda assured Slater. "You're quite safe. Mr. Blane won't hurt you, unless I tell him to. Mr. Blane, give Mr. Slater his reward. Then step outside and keep poor Mr. Holzer company, please."

"Miss Woodbine, are you sure? Maybe I . . ."

"Yes, I'm sure."

Blane stepped forward, spurs chiming. Slater watched his hand come up, and saw the pouch. Blane let it drop on the dry goods counter. The contents made a nice, rich, clanking sound.

"Gold double eagles," said Blane. "Twenty-five of 'em."

Slater was beginning to wonder if he'd live long enough to spend it.

As he passed by Slater, making for the door, Blane crossed a narrow band of moonlight slanting through the front window. Slater got a glimpse of narrowed eyes, a blade of a nose, and a thick moustache completely hiding the man's mouth. He saw something else, beneath the hard surface. The soul of a hunter of men.

Blane gone, Amanda said, "He's my father's personal bodyguard. Also, a territorial marshal."

Slater grimaced. He was getting that wanted-man feeling again, stronger than ever.

Amanda read his thoughts. "Don't worry. Mr. Blane doesn't know about you."

"What about me?"

"I overheard that man Digby talking to my father about you. About how you're wanted in Montana, for murder. Did you murder a man in Montana, Mr. Slater?"

Slater didn't say anything.

Amanda came closer, into that silver slant of moonlight. She looked a sight better than when he had last laid eyes on her. There was a bruise on her jaw, a cut above one eyebrow. These blemishes did nothing to detract from her beauty. She was too pretty, he thought, for this country. The only real flaw in her beauty were the eyes. They were haunted with dark and desperate emotion.

"I don't care what you've done in the past. I'm more interested in what you're *going* to do."

"What is that?"

"You're going after Chacon, of course. My father is forcing you to."

"You've come to thank me in advance?"

"No. I've come to make you a proposition."

"I'm listening," muttered Slater, though he strongly suspected that he wasn't going to like what he was about to hear.

"I want you to take me with you. I want to be with you when you catch Chacon. In exchange, I won't call Mr. Blane back in here. I won't inform him that you are a desperate outlaw, wanted dead-or-alive.

"How's that for a deal, Mr. Slater?"

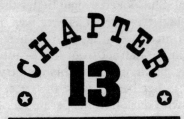

CHAPTER 13

"REVENGE," SAID SLATER. "IS THAT IT?"

"That's it exactly," snapped Amanda vehemently.

Slater shook his head. "Revenge doesn't pay, lady. Believe me, I know."

"You don't know how I feel. Don't even say you know how I feel. You couldn't possibly know."

"My parents were massacred by Indians. The Apaches took me in when I wandered south. Then I saw my Apache father murdered in cold blood by soldiers."

"And you can stand there and tell me that you

didn't want to see the men responsible pay for what they did?"

"No. What I wanted didn't make much difference. I couldn't take on the whole Sioux nation. Or the entire cavalry."

"This isn't the same. There's only one man. I should say, one animal. That's what Chacon is. An animal."

"He's an Apache warrior. And a damned smart one, too. A lot of other men, red *and* white, would have done the same."

"You sound like . . . like you're trying to defend him," she said, incredulous.

"Just statin' the cold hard, ma'am. You're actin' like Chacon's the only man who put his hands on you. That's hard to buy."

"Of course he wasn't. Some of the others. . . ." She looked quickly away, and he saw the glimmer of tears in her eyes, saw her fight to stay calm and in control. "But he was the leader. He was . . . the first. He could have kept it from happening. But he let the others have me when he was done."

"Why would he have stopped them?"

She glared hatefully at him.

"Miss Woodbine, that's why they took you along in the first place. Renegade Apaches will follow their leader only so long as he provides them with what they've got a hankering for. In this case, *Pinda-Lickoyi* men to kill, horses to steal, and women to rape. You're lucky they didn't kill you at the agency. They might have decided you weren't worth takin', that you would have slowed them down too much."

"Lucky?" The sound she made was somewhere between a laugh and a sob. "God in heaven, I wish they *had* killed me. I wish they'd shot me right between the eyes. Like they did Cameron."

"Cameron?"

"Cameron Todd. He was an inspector for the Bureau of Indian Affairs. They murdered him, and the Indian agent, Gatewell. Though I can't say that I blame them for killing Gatewell."

"What does that mean?"

"Mr. Gatewell was a dishonest scoundrel. He'd been cheating and mistreating the Indians at Cibicu Creek for years. The government provided him with supplies to distribute among the Indians at the reservation. Medicine, seed, farming tools and cattle for slaughter. He was selling most of that for his own profit. Which is why Cameron—Mr. Todd—was there. Investigating Gatewell."

Slater made a throw-away gesture. "That's been going on since the get-go."

"That doesn't make it right."

"What were you doing there?"

"I accompanied Mr. Todd. In a manner of speaking, I was responsible for the investigation."

"You?"

"Yes." She uttered a sharp, bitter laugh. "Isn't that ironic? I can scarcely believe that I was once so concerned for the welfare of the Apaches. That I made the improvement of their condition at Cibicu Creek a kind of personal crusade. Oh, I was so naive! I thought they were human beings and had the right to be treated as such."

"You can't blame all the Apache people for what a handful of renegades did to you. No more than I can blame every soldier in the United States Cavalry for murdering my Apache father."

"Don't preach to me! I hardly think that you, a bounty hunter, a man who hunts down and kills strangers for blood money, is qualified to instruct me on right and wrong."

"Maybe not. But you're not coming with me."

"I think you ought to reconsider, Mr. Slater. Your life may depend on it."

Slater fought to control his anger. She was right. He was in no position to dictate to her. She held all the cards. His only chance was to make her see reason.

"Look, if you come with me, I'll never catch Chacon. You want him dead? Fine. I'll bring his mortal remains back to you, Miss Woodbine."

"That's not good enough. I want to pull the trigger."

Slater traced the scar on his cheek with a thumb, shaking his head in wonder.

"You're not listening. If I have to drag you all over creation, I'll never catch the *cimarrones*. Savvy?"

"You won't have to *drag* me," she snapped. "I can ride. And I can shoot."

Slater sighed. "Let's say, by some miracle, we caught up with Chacon. Odds are I'll be the one ending up buzzard bait, not him. You ready, willing and able to entertain a wild bunch of Chiricahua bucks again, Miss Woodbine? What's the matter? Didn't get enough the first time around?"

He braced himself, expecting an explosion. She was a powderkeg of tightly-wound emotion, and he'd just lit the fuse.

But she fooled him. Smiled faintly.

"You can't talk me out of this. And you can't scare me out of it, either. If that happened, you'd take my life. I'd want you to."

"I would? You sure about that?"

She looked at him, like she could see through the tough exterior, into the soul and conscience of the man.

"I'm fairly certain. And if you weren't civilized enough to do it, I'd see to it myself."

Slater grunted, skeptical. "We won't have time to blink when they come at us. Usually, the first you see of an Apache is when he's killing you."

"I'm going with you," she repeated, adamant.

"Or I'm calling Mr. Blane in here to tell him about your little secret."

"What do you think your father will do when he finds out I'm taking you right back out to Chacon? I'll have your Blane feller, and probably ten more like him, on my trail."

"I can take care of that. You'll have to trust me."

Slater laughed flat out. "Sure. Like I trust lightning to strike."

"Your choice, Mr. Slater."

Thoroughly disgusted, Slater said, "You drive a hard bargain, lady."

"I am accustomed to getting what I want."

"Oh, I reckon you'll get that, sure enough."

He said it with confidence. Because he was pretty certain that deep down inside, Amanda Woodbine wanted to die.

If so, going with him after Chacon was a damned fine way to get that job done.

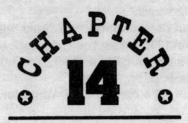

CHAPTER 14

HE WOKE BEFORE DAWN, COMING OUT OF sleep fully alert and attuned to his surroundings, as was his custom. Rolling out of the blankets spread out on the dry goods counter, he stepped lightly to the curtained doorway and listened a moment. Doc Holzer was still sleeping soundly in the back room.

Moving to the solitary front window, Slater checked the street. A stray dog was slinking into an alley between two buildings across the wide, rutted lane. The mongrel was the only sign of life in San Manuel at this early hour. The sky was dark and scattered with stars. Only a faint pearling of the eastern rim promised a new day dawning.

Slater hoped that this one would turn out better than the one before.

He slipped, quiet as a ghost, out of the general store. Making for the livery, a distant sound caused him to stop at the mouth of an alley and look to his right. Beyond the gulch of Cabrito Wash rose a scrub-covered slope crowned by the old church. Beside the church was a graveyard. Up there it was, by degrees, less dark, and he could see two men digging in the rocky soil.

A new grave, thought Slater. The final resting place of the notorious road agent and killer, Bitteroot Carson. A six-foot hole in a dusty bone orchard.

Slater knew little about the outlaw he had killed, except that Carson had been a loner and only moderately successful as a holdup man. His killing of a zealous express company gun-guard had upped the bounty on his head and brought him to Slater's attention. In a way, Carson had signed his own death warrant by ending the guard's life. Slater never hunted small change. And until now, he had never hunted someone he knew well.

Chacon would be the first in that respect. As boys they had hunted together. Slater had learned many things from Chacon: how to move across the desert without making a sound or leaving a trace. How to cross open ground without being seen. How to run all day with hardly a stop. How to wait all day in the broiling desert sun without moving an inch or making the slightest noise.

Even at an early age Chacon had excelled in all these things. Though he had never fully accepted Slater as a brother, they had been friends.

That wasn't so anymore. To Chacon, every white-eyes was an enemy. He hated them, each and every one. Man, woman and child. This, because of his father's murder at the hands of the cavalry. Chacon was *netdahe*—sworn to kill the *Pinda-Lickoyi*. In Chacon's kind of warfare there was no quarter given or expected—even to childhood friends, if they were white.

Slater trudged on through San Manuel's quiet streets, deep in thought. He had never hunted the Apache. Many times, because of his well-known expertise in desert lore, he had been asked to scout for the army. Always he had refused out of hand. In many ways the Apache were his people. His true parents had perished when he was still quite young. Too young to possess a memory of them that he could hold to. And his uncle had certainly never made him feel that any kinship existed between them.

Only Loco had shown him kindness. The other Bedonkohe had at least shown him respect and courtesy, once he had proven his worth. Because of this, he had never turned his skills against any Apache. *Reducido* or *teilcolthe*—tame Apache or renegade—they were all as one to him.

Now he was going to have to break his unwritten rule. Chacon had to die in order for him to survive. This he accepted, with a kind of stoic fatalism. He did not go after Chacon for money, or because Chacon was a bad man who had committed many atrocities against the whites—Amanda Woodbine not least of all. Slater did not take sides in the war between whites and Apaches. Right and wrong, good against evil, did not enter into the equation.

Chacon's life for his own. Simple as that. Such was the bargain, and so it would be.

To survive out here, you did what you had to do.

Never letting his guard down was one thing a man had to do to stay above snakes.

For once, passing through the 'dobe archway into the wagonyard, Slater's guard was down. He was too busy mulling over his sorry situation, the result of the troublesome events of the last couple of days, to pay due attention to his surroundings.

So he walked right into the trap, pretty as you please.

Had he been alert, he would have been forewarned. Many times before he had come to the livery in the early morning. Always there had been signs of activity. It took time to properly stoke the blacksmith forge, and the old Mexican and his strapping sons rarely wanted for business. They serviced not just San Manuel but had a maintenance contract with the express company. The quality of their workmanship was widely known.

Over beneath the pole *ramada*, the forge was cold.

The old Mexican sat with his back to the wall of the stable, chin on chest, legs splayed, and sombrero pulled down low.

Slater had crossed the yard and drawn within a half-dozen strides of the old Mexican before the warning cry of instinct pierced his moody preoccupation.

There was something very wrong with the old man.

He didn't miss a stride. Sweeping the shoulder-racked Spencer down, he reached the old Mexican and lifted the floppy brim of the sombrero with the end of the carbine's barrel.

The old man's shirt was drenched with blood. His throat had been slashed from ear to ear.

A noise behind him sent him diving to one side before he had even identified the sound. He heard the bullets striking the stable wall as he rolled. The booming of revolvers was quick to follow.

Pistol hammers being cocked. That was the

sound which had triggered a violent reaction in him.

Coming out of the diving roll and up onto one knee, Slater whipped the Schofield from its holster. There was no time for trying to line up the rifle gripped in his left hand. He fired the revolver twice even before he'd located his target, aiming in the direction of the gunshots.

A buckboard stood in the corner of the yard. A man had been hidden in the wagon bed; now he was on his feet, pistols in both hands, firing one, then the other, sending a hail of hot lead across the wagonyard at Slater.

The man was Joe Gault.

Quick reaction had saved Slater from being backshot.

With the target located, Slater adjusted his aim and fired again.

The bullet plucked at the serape worn by Joe Gault. It was a splendid shot at this distance and under these conditions, and it saved Slater's bacon. In a face-to-face gun-duel he was outmatched by a shootist like Gault. But the close call unnerved Gault, and he stopped shooting at Slater long enough to vault out of the buckboard, seeking better cover.

Slater moved at the same time, leaping for the stable doorway. Gault's next shot splintered a doorframe post scant inches from Slater's head.

Ducking for cover, Slater tripped over something and sprawled headlong.

That something was the body of one of the old Mexican's sons.

Livid marks around his neck indicated that he had been strangled. Bulging eyes, swollen, protruding tongue and a bluish cast to his complexion was testimony to the agony of his final seconds.

Slater swore under his breath, threw a wary look down the carriageway of the stables.

Where there was one Gault, there were others. They were after him. The callous bastards had murdered at least two innocent men to get at him, and he didn't doubt that they had done this deed without the slightest remorse.

That really burned Slater's powder.

CHAPTER 15

HE FIGURED HE HAD TWO OPTIONS.

One was to sit tight in the darkness of the stables and let them come for him. The other was to get out of the trap. Get out shooting. Slater preferred the second alternative. The fastest way was on horseback, and the only route was across the wagonyard. To make a run for it across the yard on foot spelled certain death.

Stalls lined either side of the stables. There were no lofts under the low-pitched pole roof, so he didn't have to worry about being jumped from above. Still, he had to count on at least one of the Gault's being somewhere in here with him. For one thing, Joe had stopped shooting. Was he afraid of hitting one or both of his brothers?

Down the row of stalls on Slater's side, a horse whickered. A board creaked.

There were three rounds left in the Schofield. He took the time to feed three more into the empty chambers. It was the wise man who loaded up whenever there was a lull in the action.

In a catfooted crouch, he moved along the stalls, the carbine still gripped in his left hand, the revolver in his right.

Up ahead, a horse snorted and bumped nervously against the slat sides of its stall.

A stall door swinging suddenly open caught him by surprise. He threw up his left arm to prevent the door from hitting him full in the face. The impact drove him backwards. Falling, he lost the Spencer.

Uttering a piercing coyote yell, Ted Gault hurtled the stall door and launched himself at Slater. He had both of his Bowie knives in play now. Ten inches of cold steel in each hand. Slater rolled out from under and Ted belly-flopped on the straw-covered hardpack. The youngest Gault was wiry and agile; he bounced right back up.

For an instant they crouched in the darkness of the stables, facing each other, not six feet apart.

"You stupid sonuvabitch," sneered Ted.

He lunged.

Slater fired once.

Straightening, Slater looked impassively down at Ted as the younger Gault's heels drummed against the hardpack, and his last ragged breath rasped in his throat.

"Stupid?" muttered Slater dryly. "Well, I ain't the one who brought knives to a gunfight."

He stepped over the dead man and into the stall where Gault had been hiding. He recognized the horse—Bitteroot Carson's dun mare.

"Bet you thought you were rid of me," murmured Slater as he backed the dun out of the stall.

In the carriageway, he grabbed a handful of mane and swung Indian-style aboard the horse. A savage gut-kick with both heels sent the dun plunging through the doorway and out into the wagonyard.

Joe Gault was right outside the stables, back to the wall, when Slater emerged. He fired both guns simultaneously. But Slater was bent down low, cheek against the dun's neck, and the bullets passed harmlessly over him.

The next two shots Joe Gault fired were aimed at the dun mare.

Slater felt the horse shudder and stumble. She didn't make a sound, and pitched suddenly sideways. Slater hit the ground with bone-jarring impact. Another bullet struck the hardpack inches from his head and spewed dirt into his eyes. He rolled over, sat up, and fanned the Schofield's hammer, firing back at Gault. Half-blind and out-gunned, it was his only chance. A desperate chance.

The hammer fell on an empty chamber.

Slater wiped a sleeve across streaming eyes. He got to his feet, shaken by the fall, automatically thumbed the loading gate open, dumped the emp-ties, and began reloading. Even with his vision blurred, he could tell that Joe Gault lay spreadea-gled and death-still on the hardpack.

He heard the lethal whisper of the bullwhip a fraction of a second before the braided rawhide tip laid open the back of his wrist. Gasping at the sear-ing pain, he lost his grip on the Schofield. The whip slashed at him again, this time slicing open sleeve and arm. He spun away.

Growling like a trap-caught lobo, Ben Gault let fly once more with the bullwhip. The rawhide snaked around Slater's neck. Gault yanked sav-agely and pulled Slater off his feet. Slater clawed at the noose of rawhide, but it was too tight around his throat, imbedded deeply into the flesh, squeez-ing his windpipe closed. He fought for air.

Laughing, Gault started to reel him in like a hooked fish, dragging him across the wagonyard.

A wave of blackness washed over Slater. He fought weakly to the surface. He could hear Gault's laughter, dimly, over the roaring in his ears—a sound like the endless thunder of a waterfall. Gault was laughing at him. That made Slater good and mad. Rage ignited one last spark of strength.

Groping over his head, Slater grasped the whip with both hands, rolled over on his belly, somehow got his legs under him and charged like a bull out of the chute.

It was a clumsy, stumbling run straight at Gault, who sidestepped and laid the long hickory handle of the bullwhip across Slater's skull. Slater went down, kicked out wildly and by sheer luck connected with Gault's legs. Gault fell. The whip slackened. Slater wasted no time removing it from around his neck. He sucked in a chestful of sweet air. He almost passed out again. Hot blood trickled down the side of his face. A couple of good, deep breaths made him feel like a new man. He found the strength to stand up.

Gault's haymaker came out of nowhere and lifted him off his feet, pounding him into the dust again.

The copper taste of blood in his mouth, Slater got up. He could, in a vague and watery way, see Gault's bulk in front of him.

"I'll kill you with my bare hands, you bastard," said Gault. "I'll snap your neck like a dry branch. I'll squeeze your skull until your brains pop out."

"Shut the hell up," muttered Slater, spitting blood, "and let's get on with it."

Gault came for him, swinging another round-house blow. Slater ducked under and delivered an uppercut to the jaw that rocked Gault on his heels. He followed this with a left jab to Gault's face. Gault tottered backwards, a look of foolish surprise on his face. Blood streamed out of both nostrils and into his spade beard.

Slater shuffled forward and launched another punch. Gault hit him first, in the breadbasket. Slater never saw it coming. All that sweet air gushed out of his lungs. He sagged to his knees, sucking wind. Gault kicked, but Slater swayed backwards, surged upright once more, Gault's leg clutched in his arms. Gault dropped heavily, fetching his head a good lick on the hardpack.

Slater let go of the leg and waited for Gault to get up, then put everything he had left into a gut-punch. Gault doubled over. Slater drove his knees up into the man's face. Gault was out cold before he hit the ground.

"Mother of God."

Slater turned, almost toppled over, planted his feet firmly, and glowered at Heck Digby through a swimming red haze.

"You next?" he growled. He wanted to kill. He had a bad case of what the Apaches called *heshke*, a homicidal craze that bordered on madness.

Digby held up a hand.

"Heard gunplay. Come to break up the party."

"Too late."

With a look around that took in the bodies of Joe Gault and the old Mexican, Digby nodded. "I see that. What in tarnal creation happened?"

"Gaults . . . waitin' for me. Killed the old man and one of his sons."

"Figured they'd want your hide, after what you done to Ted last night."

Slater fetched the Schofield out of the dust and tried to walk a straight line towards the stables.

"You leavin'?"

"Gonna stop me?" Slater looked at the scatter-gun cradled in the seedy badge-toter's arm, and tried to remember if he had reloaded the Schofield.

"Cain't. You're the governor's own personal bloodhound. For the time being, anyhow. But like I said, Slater, I got a quarrel with you. I don't forgive or forget. For us, there'll be a time and a place."

Slater looked at Ben Gault.

"You aim to lock him up? Or do I need to walk over there and put a bullet in him right here and now?"

"You'd do that, too, wouldn't you? Shoot a man to death while he's out like a dead cat?"

"Damned straight."

"I'll take care of Gault. You just ride the hell on out of my town."

"My pleasure," said Slater, and turned away.

CHAPTER 16

CROSSING THE CACTUS FLATS OF THE SAN Pedro Valley, Amanda Woodbine reached the spot where Prospect Creek came brawling out of the sierra through steep Wild Horse Canyon. The creek, nurtured by strong mountain springs, was vigorous year-round at this point; only a few miles out into the arid wasteland it would dwindle to a muddy trickle.

Amanda knew this country well. Her birthplace was but two days' ride north and east, on the banks of the Gila River. Her father had been a prosperous rancher before turning to politics, and he had carved out a cattle empire in the shadows of the Mescal Mountains.

Where the Prospect emerged from the narrow canyon was the point of rendezvous with Sam Slater that she had insisted on, less than ten miles from the hardscrabble homestead and stage stop belonging to Wink Langley.

She had covered those ten miles alone, and the journey had been more difficult than antici-pated. Her recent ordeal endured at the hands of Chacon and his brutal renegades had robbed her of her courage. Before, nothing had scared her. Now everything did. Her fragile nerves almost snapped a dozen times during the ride from Lang-ley's place. The sight of distant dust had made her tremble uncontrollably, even after she had deter-mined that it was just a wind-whipped dust devil. A jackrabbit bursting from a bunch of *guajillo*, flushed by her approach, had made her heart feel as though it would burst right out of her chest.

Plagued with self-doubt, wondering if she had the grit to see this through, she drove herself re-lentlessly on, chiding herself for her fearful imag-inings, that Chacon and his band lurked behind every saguaro and catclaw. Wasn't that what she wanted, after all? To meet Chacon one more time? To shoot him down as she would a rabid dog? Why should she be afraid? What worse thing could hap-pen to her than that which had already happened?

Chacon and his gang had raped her. She felt so degraded and dirty. So outraged. The Apaches had killed her, just as surely as they had killed Cameron.

Poor Cameron! The salty wash of bitter tears blurred her vision. She wiped fiercely at her eyes as she stopped the sturdy sorrel Langley had—against his will, admittedly—provided her. At the rim of the Prospect's wash, among the pale verde that grew here in profusion, she looked upstream, toward the mouth of the canyon.

At first she saw no sign of Slater.

"Damn you," she sobbed. "Damn you. . . ."

The sorrel whickered, smelling another horse in the vicinity. Then she saw the claybank, stepping into view beyond a cutbank a hundred yards upstream.

Relief came in a warm flood. She needed the bounty hunter. Not for protection, she told herself, but because she could never hope to track Chacon down all by her lonesome.

She angled the sorrel down the bank, let the horse pick its way along the rocky bottom beside the creek. The claybank watched their approach. Where was Slater? Surely that had to be Slater's horse.

But what if it wasn't?

The hard shape of the Winchester 44/40 felt reassuring beneath her right thigh, where the repeater rode in the saddle boot. She was about to pull the weapon out when something burst from the embankment to her right in an explosion of dirt.

The sorrel crow-hopped into the creek shallows, snorting. The cry startled out of Amanda was sharply curtailed as something struck her, knocking the wind out of her. She felt herself carried out of the saddle, and gasped at the shock of cold water as she landed in the creek.

She lashed out in blind panic until she realized that there was nobody there to lash out at. She blinked water from her eyes. Sitting in three inches of Prospect Creek, soaked to the skin, she focused on the man standing a few feet away.

"That's how much time you'll have to kill Chacon," said Slater. "Still think you can do the job?"

Befuddled, she looked past him, at the hole he had dug into the bank, at her horse, hightailing it upcreek, then back at Slater, who was caked with pale dirt from top to bottom. His brief descent into the Prospect hadn't washed off much of it.

She put it all together. He had excavated that hole, backed into it, standing almost upright, then covered himself with small rocks and dirt. Only his face, caked with more dirt, had remained uncovered.

This Slater had done at the first sign of an oncoming rider. If the rider had turned out to be someone other than Amanda, his reaction might have been more violently extreme.

Of course, she didn't know that. She assumed that he had arranged this demonstration to discourage and humiliate her.

Amanda Woodbine got good and mad.

"How dare you!" she spluttered, indignant.

"You're not hurt."

She made a quick diagnosis of her condition. While she understood, somehow, that he had shielded her in the fall, this did little to salve her feelings.

"You . . . you . . ." She couldn't think of a term abusive and derogatory enough to adequately express her opinion of him.

"Yeah," he said wryly. "I know. Let me give you a hand."

He reached out. She slapped the hand away and stood up on her own.

Slater gave her the once-over. She wore pants tucked into high boots, a shirt and vest. Her hat hung by its chinstrap down her back. Her yellow hair had been cut short, just below the ears.

"You're all dressed up like a man," he observed. "But you still smell like a woman. That pretty smell will get us both killed."

Amanda couldn't imagine how she could possibly smell pretty after ten long miles on horseback under the desert's furnace sun.

"I bathed in San Manuel, last night, if that's any of your business, *Mister* Slater. I tried to rid myself of the stench of those Apache animals. I scrubbed until my skin was raw."

"We'll have to find you a turpentine bush to roll around in, *Miss* Woodbine. 'Cause an Apache buck will pick up the scent of a white woman a mile downwind."

She shuddered and told herself that it was the cold spring water dancing out of the cool shadows of Wild Horse Canyon that made her cold.

"Just what were you trying to prove with that stunt?" she snapped.

"That you ought to go home."

"Don't start that. I'm going with you, and that's all there is to it."

Slater turned away, disgusted. Climbing the bank, he gazed out across the cactus flats, in the direction from whence she had come.

"I'm not being followed," she said irritably, wading out of the creek.

"Why not?"

"My father thinks I'm on the stage heading for Globe."

"How is it that you aren't?"

"The stage noons at Wink Langley's place. Wink's daughter, Constance, and I have been friends since childhood. When the stage stopped, I was pretending to be asleep. Mr. Blane was riding up top with the driver. He thought he was waking me to tell me that I should have something to eat. I told him that I wasn't hungry. That I just wanted to sleep. When he and the driver had gone into the common room, I slipped out and around to the back. I found Constance in the kitchen. These are her clothes. She took my place on the stage."

Slater came down off the embankment to stare at her. "Just how long you reckon that'll fool Blane?"

"He's riding up top. The stage won't stop until sundown."

Slater shook his head. "Those Langley folks will be in a heap of trouble when your father finds out."

"Wink Langley didn't know that Constance and I had changed places until the stage pulled out. He was angry. He gave me a good talking-to." She smiled smugly. "And he was going to send Jesus, his hired hand, after the stage. When Jesus had the horse saddled, and went to fill his canteen at the well, I saw my chance. I took the horse—the only horse Wink has that is broken to the saddle—and opened the corral gate to let the stage horses out."

"They didn't try to stop you?"

"Oh, they tried," said Amanda, obviously proud of herself. "But what were they to do? Shoot me?"

"I might have."

"I don't doubt that. But Wink Langley is a good and decent man."

Slater smiled. The implication that he was not a good, decent man failed to bother him. Good and decent were virtues he did not aspire to.

"They'll come after you, sooner or later. Blane. Others."

"Yes, yes, I know." She made an impatient gesture. "But don't you see? They won't know you're involved."

"They'll track you here. They'll see you met somebody."

"What's the matter? You're supposed to be the best, Mr. Slater. Can't you cover our trail? Can't you fool Blane?"

"That depends on how good he is."

"I would think, being a wanted man, that you're no stranger to throwing off posses."

Slater grimaced. So much for this turning out to be a better day, he thought.

"I told Constance I was going after Chacon alone." Amanda laughed, a somewhat shrill and unnatural laugh that made Slater uneasy. "She thought I was crazy. I could see it on her face. And she could tell that I was in earnest. When I took up the shears and cut my hair short she looked kind of terrified. She said that I was different. She didn't mean just my appearance. And she's right, you know. I am different. I'm not the Amanda Woodbine she once knew. Chacon murdered that sweet, innocent young lady."

Disgruntled, Slater turned his back on her and started up the wash, towards the claybank.

"You talk too much," he muttered.

She followed him, her eyes shooting daggers into his back.

The sorrel had stopped a short distance past Slater's horse, and was busy cropping at sparse clumps of bluegrass thrusting up through the rocks. Slater caught it up and brought it back to Amanda.

"Let's get going," he said gruffly. "I've wasted half a day waiting on you."

"At least you're still a free man," she snapped back.

Slater grunted at that and mounted the claybank.

"Which way are we going?" she asked.

Relishing her reaction to the news, he said, "The Apache reservation at Cibicu Creek."

He paused long enough to see the slow dawning of horror on her face, then spun the claybank and headed west.

CHAPTER
17

LOCKED UP IN THE SAN MANUEL JAIL, BEN
Gault slept like a baby. There wasn't much else to
do. He slept the sleep of the pure-at-heart, like a
man whose conscience had no call to bother him.

In fact, Ben Gault had never in his misspent
life been unduly bothered by conscience.

Most men in his place would not—could not—
have slept.

His brothers were dead. He was in the hoosegow, facing a murder charge. These days, there
was only one possible sentence on a conviction for
murder: hanging by the neck till dead.

Gault acccpted all this with the equanimity of

a man well-acquainted with a fact of frontier life: there were no guarantees. A man lived day to day. The chances of reaching a ripe old age were exactly two: slim and none.

The sound of the bullwhip hitting the hard-pack floor of the cell interrupted his righteous sleep.

He rolled over on the narrow, rope-slat bunk and opened one eye. The whip was coiled like a twenty-foot snake within easy reach. He didn't reach for it, though. Instead, he cast that one open eye at the wall of strap-iron in which the cell door was set.

Sheriff Heck Digby stood out in the hall that ran the length of the two-cell block.

"What am I supposed to do with that?" growled Gault. "Hang myself in here and save the taxpayers their hard-earned shinplasters?" He snorted. "Hell with that. We'll do her up right, hoss. The band, the crowd, the gallows, the whole bit."

"Want to talk to you, Ben," said Digby.

"Who's that with you?"

Another man stepped into full view. "Name's Taggert."

"Want to talk," repeated Digby bluntly. "You want to listen?"

"Ain't got nothin' better to do at the moment." Gault opened the other eye, sat up, and stretched long and noisily, like a bear fresh out of winter hibernation.

"You're in a heap of trouble," remarked the sheriff.

"Oh, hell, I know that. But my ox has been in a ditch before."

"Not a ditch this deep. Y'know that ole Mex you killed?"

"I didn't cut the old man."

"That's right. Your brother Ted did. But you done for the younger one. And he's got six brothers. All six of them together could lift a locomotive, easy. They was away on errands and such this mornin', but most of 'em are back in town now. And they want your hide sumpin fierce."

"Bring the damned bean-eaters on," growled Gault, always primed for a ruckus. "One at a time or all at once, I don't give a hoot in hell."

"If they don't kill you, you'll hang for sure," opined Taggert.

"I never hankered for dyin' in bed. And it was for a good cause that I killed the boy, you ask me. To get Sam Slater."

"That's what we want to talk about," said Digby.

Gault stood up and came to the strap-iron.

"Let's cuss and discuss, boys."

Digby edged closer and lowered his voice.

"Reckon you want Slater dead."

"He killed my brothers. What do you think?"

"We want him dead, too. Maybe you'd like to ride with us and have a hand."

Gault squinted suspiciously at the badge-toter.

"What do you got against him?"

"He's worth two thousand dollars up Montana way," said Taggert. "Dead or alive. Murdered a man there. Digby and I aim to collect."

"Is that so?"

"I get thirty dollars a month and anything I can steal and get away with," said Digby sourly. "I'll trade this piece of tin for a thousand dollars any day."

"Would you now? Then why don't you turn in your badge and go after Chacon? He's worth more than Slater."

"I ain't got nothin' against Chacon."

"I see. Or maybe you just think Slater will be easier to take? If so, not by much, Digby."

"I want the hell out of this godforsaken country, for myself," said Taggert fervently. "And Sam Slater's hide is my ticket."

Gault tugged at his beard.

"What's my cut?"

"You get to see him dead," said Digby. "And you get out of jail."

"I'll be a wanted man myself, then."

Digby shrugged. "I can't fix that. Least you'll be breathin'."

Gault paced the cell. Two strides to the back wall, two strides back. Several times he stepped over the bullwhip. Finally picked it up, coiled it with loving care, and returned to the strap-iron.

"When do we start?"

"Tonight. When it's full dark."

"Slater's gone after Chacon, you know."

Digby grimaced. He didn't relish the prospect of hard and dangerous traveling, but he had an aching desire to see Sam Slater's lamp blown out. He was hoping that Gault and Taggert could take care of the real work. That way he wouldn't have to get his fool head blown off. His job as San Manuel's law was cushy enough, and he had some regrets about chucking it. Consolation was the knowledge that a thousand pesos would set him up like a king in some little village south of the border, with maybe a pretty senorita or two to serve him mescal all day and warm his bed at night. All that and the satisfaction of knowing that he played a key role in the demise of that bastard Slater.

Yeah. It was worth it.

"You're a bounty hunter, like Slater," said Taggert. "Can't you track him?"

"Hell yes, I can track him. Can a rooster crow?" Gault laughed. "Fact is, I got me a real good notion of just how Mr. Slater aims to find Chacon."

"How's that?"

Gault abruptly stopped laughing. "I'll show you. But I ain't stupid enough to tell you. Slater knows he'll never catch Chacon if Chacon's on the run. And since he's Apache his own self—or too damned near for my taste—Slater will think like an Apache. He'll make Chacon come to him, on ground of his own choosing."

"How will he do that?"

"I'll tell you this much," said Gault slyly. "When we ride out of here tonight, boys, we're going straight to the Apache *rancheria* at Cibicu Creek."

Digby and Taggert threw sidelong glances rife with alarm at one another.

Ben Gault just tossed back his head and laughed like there was no tomorrow.

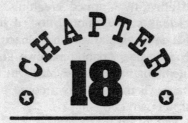

CHAPTER 18

"I'M NOT GOING DOWN THERE."

Amanda Woodbine was adamant. She was also frightened.

For the first time, she realized that she was deep in the Apache reservation. In the gray gloom that delineates night from morning, she looked down upon the Chiricahua *rancheria* in the valley below. She looked at it as one might look down into a rattlesnake hole. It was natural to feel uneasy in the presence of rattlesnakes and Apaches. You never knew for certain that all the rattlesnakes were in the hole. Or that all the Apaches were in camp. You never knew for sure that there wasn't one right behind you.

The day before, Slater had pushed hard, finally settling into a cold camp well after sunset. He had offered her beef jerky and teeth-breaking corn dodgers, but she had been too tired to eat. In fact, she hadn't had much of an appetite since her ordeal.

The offer to share his provisions was the only consideration Slater showed her. They had not spoken all day, nor did they that night. Which was fine with Amanda. She fell into a fitful sleep with the Winchester close beside her.

Slater roused her long before dawn. She awoke more exhausted than ever. In her dreams she relived every painfully unspeakable minute of her living nightmare as the captive of the Apaches. The slitted dark eyes, the fierce features, the gruff laughter, the rough hands mauling her. The empty, helpless feeling. That had been the worst part: the helplessness. No, she didn't mind a short sleep.

There was plenty of dreamless sleep in the grave.

They had traveled many miles before the first streak of pearl gray touched the eastern rim of the sky. Tough miles through rough country: steep rides and deep canyons and boulder fields. Country that was hard on horse and rider. Country

suited only to rattler, gila monster, scorpion and
Apache.

Until they arrived at this high granite table,
where wind-twisted cedar and patches of bea-
vertail cactus grew somehow in the cracks and
crevices, Amanda had not realized how far they
had come—or exactly where they were.

Now she knew. Looking down at the cluster of
beehive-shaped *jacales* in the valley below her,
where smoke from morning cookfires hovered in
a haze above the village, she wondered if she could
stand being so close to *them* again.

"I'll go to pieces if I even see another Apache,
she thought.

"I don't care what you do," said Slater. "That's
where I'm headed."

"Chacon isn't down there," she said testily.
"You're wasting time here and he's probably clear
to the border by now."

"I don't reckon I want to eat his dust all the
way to the Cima Silkq," he snapped right back at
her. "He'd come sneakin' back here sooner or
later. I just aim on makin' it sooner."

"What are you going to do?"

"Come with me and find out."

Wide-eyed, she looked down into the valley
again.

"No. No, I'll wait here."

"I won't be back until tonight, lady. Sure you want to stay out here all by your lonesome?"

His sarcastic tone cut to the quick. Her glare was a slow burn.

"I'd rather that then spend the entire day and night with those . . . those . . ."

"Animals? Suit yourself."

He neck-reined the claybank into a turn.

"Slater."

He checked the horse and looked at her.

"The agency can't be more than five miles down the valley. After what happened, I'm sure I'd find a detachment of troops and Indian scouts there."

"I reckon so. They're usually where they're needed a day late and a dollar short."

"If you don't come back, I'll go tell them about you. I swear it."

Slater drew a long breath, then touched his heels to the claybank and moved on through the wind-sculpted cedars.

She watched him until he was out of sight. He never once looked back.

The Apache camp seemed to slumber in the lee of sheer granite crags streaked with the vivid pink of sunrise until Slater reached the valley floor and pointed the claybank across a dusty sage-brush flat in the direction of the *rancheria*. All of a sudden the Apaches emerged from their *jacales* and *ramadas*, swarming like ants out of a disturbed colony. In short order, two men, mounted on the wiry desert mustangs the Apache favored, came galloping towards the lone *Pinda-Lickoyi*.

As they drew near, trailing plumes of dust that hung in the still air and caught the first slanting rays of the rising sun, Slater checked the claybank and waited for them to close ground.

They rode circles around him for a moment, yelping like happy coyotes, brandishing the short Apache lances above their heads. Slater sat his saddle and watched them with a bored expression.

In olden days, when rifles and ammunition were in abundance, supplied by gunrunners in flagrant violation of government ordinance, this pair would have fired a dozen or so rounds into the air. Now, though, a man could probably count the number of guns in working order possessed by the *reducidos* at Cibicu Creek on the fingers of one hand. The Apaches were truly a defeated people, and in a way it depressed Slater to see this.

With or without guns to sky-shoot, these two young men were determined to intimidate Slater. They failed. He had expected just such a greeting. If he reacted in a hostile manner they would kill him, and be well within their rights. The reservation was Apache land where Apache rules applied.

Slater let them raise a curtain of choking dust and yell themselves hoarse for a full minute.

"*Enjuh!*" he barked. "Good! That's enough. Time to stop playing games like little *ish-ke-nes.*"

The Apaches brought their snorting mustangs under control and sat glaring at Slater, one on either side of the manhunter.

"This one does not know these two Bedonkohe," said Slater.

"Nazati would like to know who this white-eyes is, who thinks he can come uninvited to our camp."

This came from the brave to Slater's left, speaking not to Slater, but rather to his *compadre.* It was unforgivably rude to ask a man his name directly, and Nazati would not degrade himself in such a fashion, even if the stranger was a white man.

"Yes," agreed the other. "That is something Ca-do would also like to know."

"Slater. *Ugashe*—go. Ask your fathers if they do not know me."

He saw that the name had meaning for Nazati, who boldly kicked his horse forward to peer, at close quarters, at the purple scar on Slater's sun-darkened cheek.

"It is Scar!" Nazati cried out to Ca-do. "Go and tell Natannae that Loco's white son is here."

"*Hoo-hoo-ay!*" yelled Ca-do, and his mustang

took off with a quick jackrabbit-leap off bunched-up hind legs, to go thundering back towards camp, and the throng of Apaches waiting and watching from its outskirts.

"Nazati has heard of Scar," said the Chiricahua who remained. "Scar is a brother to the Bedonkohe. Nazati cannot help but wonder if Scar has brought *na-to*, and *tu-dishishn*, for his Bedonkohe brothers."

Slater bit down on a sharp rebuke. The young Apache was as close to begging for tobacco and "black water"—coffee—as the remnants of Chiricahua pride would permit. This disturbed Slater. Nazati looked thin and underfed. He wore only breechclout and desert moccasins. And the brass reservation tag on a rawhide thong about his neck.

They are numbered and tagged like cattle at a slaughterhouse, thought Slater. He turned his eyes away.

He couldn't blame Chacon and his handful of renegades for preferring death on the war trail to the dishonor of agency prison.

The lookout he had killed on the hill above Ghost Springs—*that* had been a true Chiricahua Apache, mused Slater. Nazati was not worthy to stand in that one's shadow.

"*Callate*—come," urged Nazati, suddenly more formal, sensing, perhaps, Slater's displeasure. "Scar will be welcome in the *che-wa-ki* of the Bedonkohe."

With a curt nod, Slater kicked the claybank into a canter, and rode alongside Nazati toward the camp.

He felt confident that after he did what he had come to do, Loco's white son called Scar would never again be welcome.

CHAPTER 19

THE BEDONKOHE GATHERED AROUND SLA-
ter as he and Nazati entered the village. The entire
camp was curious about the lone white rider. Curious and wary. Wary, because too many times the
white man had come calling and brought bad news
to the Apache. Curious, because many of them
wondered, as had Nazati, what gifts the white man
carried. The white man always brought gifts. Especially when he also bore bad tidings.

The camp stood in the ox-bow curve of a rocky
creek tumbling out of the mountains. The horses
of the Bedonkohe herd were on loose graze in the
sparse, sun-browned grass of the valley floor. A

few acres of miserable-looking cornfields and melon patches could be seen near the creek, the source of their irrigation. With the exception of the Aravaipa sub-tribe, Apaches were mediocre farmers at best. Their hands better fitted the hilt of the knife than the handle of a hoe.

But the warrior days were over. The Apaches had fought the U.S. army for forty long years. They had held out longer, and given the yellow-leg soldiers more hell, than any other tribe of Indians in the West. So many years of war took a heavy toll. Never many to begin with, they were now too few to carry on the good fight. Slater searched the dark, impassive faces on either side of him as he rode through the camp, and recognized only a few from his years among the Bedonkohe.

All Apache *che-wa-kis* were pitched around a large circle of open ground. Into this Slater rode, Nazati beside him, the fifty-odd *reducidos* coming along behind on foot.

On the western rim of this open circle, a *jacale* somewhat larger than the rest stood apart from the others, facing east. The deerhide door-hanging was swept aside and an old man, white-haired, emerged. He wore a breechclout and *n'deh-b'keh*, leggings on horse-warped legs, a calico shirt, and a red-striped, brown Mexican blanket neatly folded and draped over his left shoulder. An amulet of jade set into hammered silver hung by a thong around his neck. His face, with its wide nose, high cheekbones, and slitted eyes, was creased with half-a-thousand lines.

This one Slater recognized. Natannae, chief of the Bedonkohe Chiricahua. Loco's brother, and so uncle to the white Apache known as Scar.

"*Buenos dias, jefe,*" said Slater. "It does Scar's heart good to see his uncle in fine health."

The harsh set of Natannae's knife-slit mouth eased into a warm smile. He came forward and put a gnarled hand on Slater's leg.

"Scar! *Bienvenido, schichobe.* Welcome, good friend. All the Bedonkohe welcome you."

With this, Natannae guaranteed that Slater would be treated with the utmost courtesy by his people. Slater's conscience started to bother him something fierce. He was going to abuse Natannae's hospitality; repay the old chief's friendship with betrayal.

He reminded himself that there was no other way to get Chacon. He had no choice.

"Come," said Natannae. "We will talk."

"*Gracias, jefe.*"

Slater dismounted, unbuckled his gunbelt, and draped it over the biscuit of his saddle. This demonstrated his trust in the Apaches. A man did not need to go armed into his own home.

Untying the saddlebags, Slater carried them into Natannae's *jacale,* following the old chief.

The walls of the dwelling were draped with blankets and deerskins. More of the same covered the floor. In the center, rimmed with stones, was a curl-leaf fire, slow-burning and smokeless. A woman was grinding corn in a *metate*.

"*Estune, ugashe!*" barked Natannae. "Woman, leave us."

They sat across the morning fire from one another. Natannae offered Slater honey water from the maguey plant, and a paste bread made from acorns and mesquite seeds. Slater wasn't hungry, but accepted, like a good guest. He opened the saddlebags and brought forth his gifts. A pound sack of Peaberry coffee, a block of Lobo Negro tobacco, an airtight container of canned milk. Natannae's eyes lit up. He shook the can, listening with delight to the slosh of its contents.

"Iron cow!" he exclaimed, delighted.

Slater laughed. "Iron cow, it is."

Natannae set the can aside, picked up the tobacco and bit off a quid. He set an enameled pot of water on the fire stones. While he waited for the water to heat for coffee-making, he studied the bruise on Slater's jaw, and the livid marks left by Ben Gault's bullwhip on his neck.

"What brings Scar back to the Bedonkohe?"

"There are some folks want me to go after Chacon. They wouldn't take no for an answer. They tried some hard persuadin'."

Natannae nodded soberly. "Scar will not hunt the Apache. *Enjuh.* Good. That is as it should be."

Then and there, lying bald-faced to Natannae, Slater had a pretty poor opinion of himself. He tried his best not to let the inner turmoil show. This was a fine time, he mused, to start entertaining principles.

He realized that Natannae was expecting more from him—more by way of explanation. Slater's instincts warned him to come clean about Amanda Woodbine.

"Scar travels with a woman," he said. "She waits up on the high divide to the east."

"*Anh*—yes. Natannae already knows this. Scar's *ish-son* is welcome also."

"Well, she ain't exactly Scar's woman. But she doesn't care for Apaches. That's certain. She's had . . . bad experiences. Scar hopes that no Bedonkohe gets too close. She has *pesh-e-gar.*"

Natannae lifted an eyebrow at that. A woman permitted to keep and use a rifle was a notion foreign to an Apache.

"She will be left alone. We all know what it is to have had bad experiences."

Slater nodded grimly. He sensed that the chief was referring to Loco. They sat in somber silence for a moment, sharing grief for the loss of one who had been close to both of them. No more would be said on the subject. Loco was dead. His name could not be spoken.

The water in the pot began to hiss. Natannae opened the pouch of coffee and dropped several handfuls into the water. He breathed deeply the aroma lifting in the steam.

"*Hijo!*" he exclaimed. "This is a rare gift."

"Scar has heard that the agent, Gatewell, stole the supplies that the government provided for the Bedonkohe."

With some satisfaction, Natannae said, "Gatewell's days of stealing are over forever."

"Was this the reason Chacon jumped the reservation?"

"There are many reasons for an Apache warrior to strike out. Natannae tried to stop him. But Chacon would not listen. Chacon burned with the *hesh-ke*, the urge to kill. He swore to kill as many white-eyes as he was able. He has become *net-dahe.* Sworn to kill his enemies until he himself is killed." Natannae shook his head. "Chacon will never return. Natannae knows this in his heart. He did not need the *diyi* to read it in the sticks. Chacon even closed his ears to the warnings of the medicine man."

"He will never return," agreed Slater. "The territorial governor has put a price on his head. The land swarms with men who want to get rich by putting a bullet in Chacon's heart."

"Chacon's heart is stone. His woman died of a sickness. There was no medicine. Gatewell sold all the medicine. The *diyi* tried his spells and potions, but they are useless against a white man's sickness."

The news hit Slater like a mule's kick.

"Huera is dead?"

Natannae scowled. In his shocked dismay, Slater had forgotten his Apache upbringing, and spoken aloud the name of a dead person.

"*Anh,*" said the Bedonkohe chief severely. "And so, in a way, is Chacon. The need for revenge blinded him, so that he forgot his duty as a father."

"A father?" echoed Slater.

"Scar has been away too long. Chacon has a daughter. Today is a special day for her. She prepares for the Sunrise Dance, when a girl-child comes of age, becomes *nah-lin*, a maiden. It is sad that Chacon will not be here to see this."

"A daughter," muttered the bounty hunter.

"We will go, and Natannae will show Chuana to Scar. But first, we will drink black water."

Natannae, eager for his first taste of coffee, lifted the pot away from the fire and reached for two small, tin cups. Slater's eyes followed him, but the manhunter wasn't really paying attention.

He was pondering the imponderable; how Fate sometimes jumped right into a man's life and started yanking on the strings. When that happened, a man had no choice but to dance to the tune or leave the shindig altogether.

He had come all this way to kidnap Chacon's wife. When word of this outrage reached the renegade leader, Chacon would come after Slater with a vengeance.

But Huera was dead.

Chacon's daughter was preparing for the ritual of *goo-chitalth*, the passage from childhood to womanhood. Tonight, then, she would go to the top of a mountain, or to a remote cave, where she would present herself to the spirits for their approval and blessing. She would be alone except for a wise woman, who would serve as escort and witness.

A perfect time, thought Slater, for the commission of the crime he had come here to commit.

CHAPTER 20

SLATER MOVED LIKE A SHADOW IN THE night, and made as much noise.

He climbed the steep, granite backbone with the effortless agility of a mountain cat. His lungs were strong, his legs like steel. The Apache desert moccasins he wore made no sound against the rock. A cool nightwind whispered in his ears. Below him, a thousand feet down in the valley, he could see pinpricks of light in a black void. Fires in the distant Bedonkohe village. Above him, the steep spine rose to meet a flat ledge cluttered with boulders. The orange light from a wind-whipped fire up there danced upon the rock facets.

Briefly, he paused to listen. Way off in the high sierra, a coyote howled a lonesome lament. There was no time to waste, and he pressed on, tireless. In five smokes, maybe less, the moon would appear above the rimrock of the eastern divide. The moon would be three-quarters full, and on such a clear night would give off much light. Like the thief that he was, Slater relied on the darkness as his most valuable ally.

Reaching the ledge, he slipped through the boulders that were strewn across it like massive pieces on some primordial chessboard.

He saw Chuana first, through the jumbled boulders. She was kneeling on a buckskin pad. A single eagle feather lay before her. She looked into the crackling fire as if in a trance. Jingles of tin and small stones had been sewn to the fringe of her buckskin dress. The abalone shell pendant on her forehead symbolized Changing Woman, mother of all Apache women.

Slater wasted a full minute gazing at her, having second thoughts. She was quite pretty, her face not nearly as broad and coarse-featured as those of many Apache women. Her large eyes were soft and brown, like a doe's. Her black hair was heavy with cattail pollen, and looked from here as golden as Amanda Woodbine's. All day today, the people of the village had gone to her and sprinkled a handful of the pollen on her head. This was a traditional blessing, always accompanied by a silent prayer for her life to be a long and happy one.

He could see her firelit features clearly from where he crouched, for she faced east. She was here to greet the rising sun, and so begin in earnest the ritual of the Sunrise Dance, a very sacred and solemn occasion for an Apache girl of fourteen.

Slater drew a long breath. By disrupting the ceremony, he was about to ruin Chuana's life. Any bad happening during the ritual would mark her for the rest of her days. Great care was taken to prevent any evil-thinking person from coming in contact with her.

No one had counted on Sam Slater presenting a threat to her.

To keep those with impure thoughts away from Chuana was particularly the responsibility of the *gouyan*, the wise woman of the village. Slater knew that the *gouyan* was nearby. It was she who fed the fire and kept it burning brightly.

Finding the wise woman was not difficult. Slater could smell the acrid smoke of her oak leaf cigarette. This scent led him right to her. She was gray-headed and wizened, her frail frame wrapped in a blanket. Slater remembered her from many years ago. Even then she had looked a hundred winters old.

Sitting among the boulders, sheltered from

the wind, she kept a watchful eye on Chuana, and smoked her Apache cigarettes.

Though he hated to do it, Slater crept up behind her and, clamping one hand over her mouth, clutched her throat with the other. His fingers sought, found and pressed the main artery. He was very precise. As she slumped over, he caught her in his arms and let her down gently. The smoldering cigarette fell in her lap. He picked it up and flicked it away.

Slater bent down low over her. In the Apache tongue, he whispered, "Scar is truly sorry, *anciana.*"

Taking the lengths of rawhide from his belt, he tied her hands and feet, working fast.

Her back to him, Chuana showed no indication that she was aware of what was happening thirty feet behind her.

Slater took the bandanna from around his neck and gagged the old woman. He felt bad about treating her this way. But he couldn't afford to let her alert the village below with her cries.

With the old woman's blanket in hand, Slater left the boulders and stepped into the opening where Chuana knelt awaiting the dawn.

He was two strides from her when she rose and turned to face him in one fluid, graceful motion.

Fear flashed in her eyes, but only briefly. She

was, after all, Chacon's daughter, and grand-daughter to the great war-chief, Loco. Though a mere girl, she had the courage and fiery pride of a warrior. Inexplicably, Slater was proud of her.

"You are Scar," she said. "What are you doing here?" She glanced past him. "Where is Sasabe? What have you done to her?"

"She will live, Chuana."

"What do you want?"

"You're coming with me."

She took one step back, then another. "No."

"Don't try to run. Scar does not want to hurt you."

She looked around. Slater thought she was picking the best route for an escape attempt, and set himself to lunge. But he misjudged her.

Seeing the stone a few feet to her right, Chuana jumped for it. Slater jumped, too, and almost got his skull split. She was lithe and quick. He was just a shade quicker. Dodging the flung stone, he threw a stiffarm that sent her sprawling, then pounced on her. She kicked and flailed, but didn't cry out. A balled fist caught him solidly on the chin. He tried to pin her arms. She was strong, stronger than he had expected. And slippery as a river eel.

She writhed and wriggled and somehow managed to slip out from under him. He was lunging for her again when she spun around and kicked him right between the legs.

The agony and hot, swirling nausea sent Slater staggering.

Seeing her chance, Chuana broke for the boulders and the darkness at the edge of the fire's light. Making a remarkable recovery, Slater dove and tackled her. Again she turned on him, snarling like a wild animal trapped in a snare. He blocked one blow, another, and another. That was about all he was going to put up with. He had a good grip on one slim ankle. Giving her leg a hard pull, he dragged her closer, bulled through her flying fists and snaked one arm around her chest. He squeezed so tight that all the air in her lungs came out in a loud whoosh! The iron-laced fingers of his free hand throttled her, feeling for the carotid artery, and pressed.

She never stopped fighting him. Her struggles began to lessen. In a moment she was out cold.

Slater let her down gently. Standing over her, he ruefully rubbed his chin.

No question, she had Chacon's blood in her veins.

Taking the clasp knife from his pocket, he knelt and cut away her dress. Fetching the blanket he had dropped during the struggle, he cut a hole in it, dead-center. He managed to hold her up in a sitting position and pull the blanket-turned-serape over her head. The dress, with all the noisy jingles, was going to remain behind.

He draped her limp body over his shoulder and went back to the wise woman. Squatting beside her, he slapped her cheeks gently. Eventually her eyes opened.

"*Enjuh*," said Slater. "That's good, *anciana*. Hear me well. Remember my words. Send riders after Chacon. There are some down there in the *che-wa-ki* who know where he is going. Have this message taken to him.

"Tell Chacon that if he wants his daughter back, he will find her in the place called Diablo. He knows the place. Scar will give him seven days. At daybreak of the eighth, he must speak Chuana's name no more. *Comprende?*"

Her dark eyes blank, the old woman nodded once.

Slater rose and vanished into the night with Chuana.

·CHAPTER·
21

SLATER FOUND THE CLAYBANK RIGHT where he had left it, hidden in a barranca near the foot of the sloping backbone of granite.

Unlashing the rope from his saddle, he tied one end around the slender waist of the still-unconscious Chuana. Then he bound her hands behind her with the same rope. The other end of the rope he secured around his own waist. He lifted her belly-down across the saddle. Untying the reins from around a large, flat rock, he led the claybank up the steep bank of the barranca before getting into the saddle himself.

He crossed the valley of Cibicu Creek two

miles south of the Bedonkohe village. The moon had risen, inundating the sagebrush and ocotillo of the flats he traversed with liquid silver. He wasn't worried about moonlight any longer. The kidnapping of Chuana would likely remain undiscovered until sunrise, when Chuana's godparents would ascend to the ledge to escort her back down to the *che-wa-ki* and a day of ritual.

Slater could well imagine the outrage that Natannae and his people would express at his misdeed. He would never be forgiven for what he had done this night. An Apache never forgot a wrong done to him.

In so many words, he had indicated to the *gouyan* that Chuana would die at daybreak eight days from now. This was an empty threat. He had no intention of harming the girl. Of course, the Apaches had no way of knowing that. They would expect the worst. They would expect him to be as merciless as they would be in the same situation. Chuana's knife-slashed buckskin dress would convince them that Slater meant to have his way with her while she lived.

Slater had no real interest in Chuana in that respect. He enjoyed women as much as the next man, but preferred them to be willing participants. Besides, he was too preoccupied with trying to stay alive to concern himself with such things right now.

Reaching the other side of the valley, he ascended the high ground and, an hour after leaving the barranca, found the granite table where he had parted company with Amanda Woodbine.

He had left the Bedonkohe village just prior to sunset, heading north. Several miles later, convinced that no one was following, he had circled back around to the vicinity of the ledge where Chuana was awaiting the dawn. The location of the ledge had been easy enough to learn during his visit in the village.

More than once he had contemplated leaving Amanda Woodbine behind. The certainty that she would carry out her threat to alert the soldiers who were sure to be at the nearby agency had prevented him from putting that thought into action. As much as he disliked her, he was stuck with her.

He checked the claybank often to listen and study the moonshadows among the wind-sculpted cedars and man-tall patches of prickly pear. If she was still up here waiting on him, Amanda would be as jumpy as a wet dog. The last thing he needed now was to get shot, accidental-like. Chances were that he would manage to get shot on purpose in the very near future.

Eventually he heard the whicker of a horse somewhere up ahead. Dismounting, he walked the claybank forward. When he heard the snicker of the Winchester's lever action, he froze.

"Don't shoot, dammit," he whispered fiercely.

A bootheel scraped rock. Limbs rustled. She emerged from a clump of cedar thirty feet in front of him. He went on up to her. She was trembling. The night wind had a cold bite at this elevation, and she had not dared to build a fire. It wasn't just the chill that had her shivering, though. Slater got close enough to see by her expression that her time alone up here had taken a heavy toll.

Amanda saw the rope tied around his waist. Her haunted eyes followed the rope to the body of the girl draped over the saddle. Stepping closer, she saw the bare legs protruding from the serape-blanket. Turning on him, she had the Winchester leveled from the hip.

"What have you done, you bastard?" she hissed.

"What do you care?" snapped Slater, reckless. "They're just animals, remember?"

"Is she dead?"

"No. She wouldn't be much use to me dead."

Amanda misconstrued that remark.

"Cut her loose. How dare you! You make me wait up here alone—you waste all this time—just so you can go down there and steal yourself a woman. Not even a woman; she's just a child. You're no better than an Apache, Slater. Let her go, or so help me I'll shoot you."

Slater was in a foul mood. He had done things

tonight that did not sit well. He was not of a mind to put up with Amanda Woodbine and her too-quick conclusions.

So he stepped right up to her, until the repeater's barrel was an inch from his chest. With a quick, savage motion, he grabbed the barrel with his free hand—he still had hold of the claybank's reins with the other—and shoved. Amanda lost her balance. As she fell backwards, he wrenched the rifle out of her grasp. She sat down hard.

"Look, lady," he rasped. "Next time you point a gun at me you had damned well better pull the trigger."

She stood up, glaring resentfully.

"I thought you were a white man, at least. With a thread of common decency. I was wrong."

Slater laughed bitterly.

"Out here, red or white, a man does what he has to do. You might just keep this in mind, Miss Woodbine. I wouldn't be here at all except for you and your father backing me into a corner. I wouldn't have to go through this, and do things I got no hankerin' to do, just to catch Chacon."

"Oh, so I'm to blame for this?" She made an angry gesture at the Apache girl.

"You could put it that way. This is Chacon's daughter. Know what that means? It means Chacon will cross hell and high water to get her back, and to kill me for taking her like this. That's the only way I know to get him in my sights. He'll be eating fire and spitting smoke. He might just get a little careless. One mistake and he's dead. Isn't that what you want? What the hell do you care *how* it's done as long as it's done?"

She looked at Chuana, digesting this information, confused by her feelings. Yes, she wanted Chacon dead. But she didn't want another woman to suffer.

"Still," she said weakly, "it isn't right."

"Right is what works. Now get on your horse. We'd better have some miles behind us come daybreak."

Sullen and tight-lipped, she brushed past him. Slater followed, leading the claybank. When he saw the sorrel he got angry all over again.

"You haven't even unsaddled your damned horse," he muttered, aggravated.

With sharp, angry motions, she untied the sorrel's reins from a cedar's shaggy trunk.

"I thought I might have to get away in a hurry."

Slater handed her the Winchester.

"You're gonna have a nice long walk to Diablo if that animal gets sore-backed."

"Diablo? Where is that?"

Slater climbed aboard the claybank, Chuana's limp body in front of him.

"End of the road for Chacon," he said. "Or us."

• CHAPTER 22 •

REACHING THE RIM OF THE HILLS JUST EAST of the agency, Ben Gault looked down at the sun-baked scatter of mudbrick and cedar-pole buildings. He sensed that all was not well.

"Hold up," he barked as Digby and Taggert, half-blind from exhaustion, started to ride their lathered mounts right on by and down the rugged slope of rock and cactus.

Digby looked numbly at the buckskin-clad manhunter.

"What's wrong?"

"I ain't sure. But somethin' ain't up to snuff. That's a guaranteed natural fact."

Digby squinted at the agency below. The place swarmed with activity.

There had to be at least a full company of horse soldiers down there. He could see the pitched tents and picket lines. He could also make out what appeared to be a congregation of Apaches, sitting in front of the largest building, the agency store. This bunch seemed to be the focus of attention for Apache scouts—easily distinguished by their army tunics—who stood in small groups all around the other Indians.

"Wonder what's going' on?" he muttered.

"Ya'll stay here," said Gault. "I'll go see what I can find out."

"Fine with me," said Taggert, who groaned as he dismounted, stiff-legged and butt-sore.

Gault moved on down the hill.

Taggert and Digby sat in the shadows of their spent horses and shared a bottle of mescal that Digby had thought to bring along. They were too tired even to bitch about how tired they were. Neither had much recent experience with hard riding. Gault had prodded them all through the night and into the day without slacking. Digby had fond recollections of his jail-front rocking chair.

They sat on the hill, suffering from the hellish heat, with nary a word passed between them, for a full hour. In spite of his aches and pains, Digby was dozing off when he heard a horse coming.

Being so uncomfortably near Apaches, Digby panicked and went for the scattergun hanging from the pommel of his saddle by a rope sling.

"Ease off," said Taggert. "It's Gault."

By the scowl on Gault's bearded features, Digby could guess he was bearing bad news.

"We missed the sonuvabitch," growled Gault.

"What? Who?" Digby was so fatigued that his mental processes—never anything to write home about—had passed into coma.

"Who the hell we been chasin' all across Hell's backyard?"

"Slater. He's been here?"

"Been and gone." Gault, still sitting his horse, uncapped his canteen, took in a mouthful of brackish water, swilled and spit. "He's done just what I figured him to do. What I'd've done myself, was I in his moccasins."

"You gonna let us in on it?" asked Taggert.

"Sure. We're partners, ain't we?" Gault leered at him. "Just about every damned, tame copper-belly on the reservation is down there. Led by the big augur hisself, Natannae. They're mad enough to spit nails. Seems Slater rode into their village yesterday, all friendly like. Then, sometime last night, he kidnapped Chacon's daughter."

"I'll be damned," muttered Taggert.

"Ain't we all? A bunch of 'em took out after him

at sunrise, but they lost his trail right quick. Which don't surprise me, it bein' Sam Slater."

"You knew he'd come here and do this, didn't you?" asked Taggert.

"Made sense to me. Slater knows that Chacon's probably south of the border now. On his way to the Sierra Madre hideouts the Apaches have used for years, if he ain't already there. He also knows that there'll be some who stayed behind on the reservation who have a real good idea where Chacon's favorite hidey-holes be. So he rides in, bold as brass, and makes off with Chacon's own flesh-and-blood."

"Who told you this?" asked Digby, by nature suspicious of all things.

"Yellow-leg lieutenant. He and I used to do a little dealin' when I was in the scalp business."

Digby grimaced. He did not care to know more about Gault's bloody enterprises.

" 'Pears that Slater told Natannae's bunch to get word to Chacon that he had seven days to meet Slater at a place called Diablo. Or else the girl dies."

"Diablo? Where's Diablo?" asked Taggert.

"I reckon I know the place he means." Gault offered no more on that subject.

"Think they'll send word to Chacon?"

"Yeah. Already done. Coupla messenger boys sent out separate, each of 'em with a string of five strong desert cayuses. They'll ride one horse to death, then jump aboard the next even as the first one goes down. They won't stop riding 'til they get where they're going." Gault screwed up his face as he performed some mental calculations. "Even if Chacon is already deep in the Sierra Madre, he'll have enough time to reach the meet with Slater."

Taggert snorted. "Slater's crazy. What's he think, that he can take on the whole bunch of Apaches single-handed? Or did he tell Chacon to come alone?"

"He didn't, 'cause he knows Chacon wouldn't. And if I had money to bet on the outcome, I wouldn't put it on the Indians."

"You make it sound like he's the greatest thing since shortbread," complained Digby.

"He's damned good at what he does. Won't make no bones about that." Gault grinned like a small dog with a big bone. "He's pert near as good as me."

"Well, you don't exactly think your shit stinks, do you, Mister Gault?" asked Taggert crossly. He was seeing his dreams of collecting big reward money drift away like dust in a tall wind.

Gault failed to take offense. He was busy plotting his next move.

"Besides," he said, "Slater ain't alone. He met up with another rider on the high ground above the Bedonkohe village. The bucks Natannae sent out after him saw that much, right before they lost the trail."

"That's just fine and dandy," muttered Digby. "He's got help now."

Gault looked down at San Manuel's ex-badge-toter with ill-disguised contempt.

"Don't like the odds, Digby? You can pull your freight for Jericho any time you're of a mind."

"And go where? I damned well cain't go back to San Manuel, after lettin' you out of jail."

"Ain't my fault. It was your idea. You did it, now you got to stand in it."

"Is the army going after Slater?" asked Taggert.

"That's what Natannae wants. The lieutenant says it's likely. They don't want the entire Chiricahua tribe goin' on the warpath. Not that the blue-bellies will try very hard. Everybody knows why Slater took the girl. To get Chacon. After all, that's what the army wants: Chacon dead, or in chains. Way I see it, if Slater does manage to get Chacon, all will be forgiven. He'll be a big hero. If he don't, and something happens to the girl, there won't be a hole this side of hell that Slater will be able to hide in."

"So what do we do?" asked Digby.

"We get there first. 'Cause there seems to be some confusion down yonder 'bout exactly where this Diablo is. Slater knows, and he seems to think

Chacon knows, too. And I know. So we got us an edge. If we push hard we might get there before Slater, seein' as how he's got to worry about his backtrail, and we don't."

"Push hard," echoed Digby, feeling immensely sorry for himself. "I'll be dead before the Apaches or Slater even get a chance to kill me."

"Fine," said Gault. "That'll make my split bigger. I aim to collect on Slater *and* Chacon, hoss. So let's ride. We're burning daylight."

He kicked his horse into a gallop, leaving them eating dust.

Taggert and Digby crawled back up into their saddles and followed.

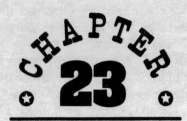

CHAPTER 23

FOR AMANDA WOODBINE, THE NEXT THREE days were one endless torment, both physically and emotionally.

Slater was without mercy. He did not seem to be the least bit concerned for the welfare of the women, or for his own. Only their horses received any consideration from him. They stopped during the day only when the horses needed a cinch-loosened breather, or a taste of water poured out of a canteen and into his hat. On numerous occasions he made everyone walk, just to save the horses.

For all the agonizing miles they put behind

them, it didn't appear to Amanda as though they were making any progress. They could go all day, from before sun-up to well after sundown, and a far-off mountain range, cobalt-blue in the distance, that she might spy away off ahead of them in the morning wouldn't look to be an inch closer at sunset.

Though born to this country, Amanda had never endured its uncompromising harshness in these terms. Her cross-country treks had always been excursions, not tests of endurance. She had never gone so far so fast for so long.

She began to long for this place called Diablo. She had no idea what or where it was, but she started to think of it as the pot of gold at the end of a rainbow. Reaching Diablo would mean that this nightmare journey was over. That she might die at Diablo didn't bother her in the least, or make her wish to postpone in any way her arrival there.

That Slater didn't make a beeline for this place aggravated her no end. They never seemed to travel for very long in the same direction. At first, she didn't believe there was rhyme or reason to the route he chose. He picked the most difficult passage more often than the easiest and most logical. He would lead them south across a sandy flat, and then, when they reached rocky ground, suddenly veer off at right angles and go on for miles before turning south again.

The first day, he doubled back at least a dozen times. He paid close attention to their backtrail. That first day he was forever putting rawhide "boots" on the hooves of the horses, then removing them some miles later. The boots were just patches of hide tied around the cannons of the horses with piggin strings. Thus covered, the steel-shod hooves made no mark on rocky ground.

Eventually she realized that he was using the terrain, and how difficult following their sign would be. This understanding, however, did little to ease the ache in her bones, or the throbbing of her head under the hammering sun, the burning of her eyes, the parched condition of her throat, the raw saddle sores on the tender flesh of her inner thighs.

She admired Slater's stamina—and hated him for it, too. No water, no food, no rest, no shade, no privation seemed to afflict him.

The Apache girl, by all appearances, was as durable as the bounty hunter. When they were riding, she rode in front of Slater. Amanda assumed that she was naked beneath the blanket-serape, and couldn't imagine how she bore so stoically the chafing of the saddle. When they walked she did so barefooted, across sand and rock so hot that Amanda could feel the heat through the thick soles of her boots. But Chuana made no complaint, displayed no weariness or pain.

They stopped the first night at a *tinaja*, a rock tank holding spring water. The western sky was aflame with sunset's vivid scarlet. The land was dark, the saguaros standing silhouetted against the painted heavens. The shallow water in the tank reflected the sky's color, and resembled a pool of blood.

Once again Slater offered Amanda dried beef and corn dodgers. This time she accepted. She had not eaten in three days, since leaving San Manuel on the morning stage to Globe. Last night, above the valley of Cibicu Creek, she had been hungry but without food, having fled Wink Langley's place without provisions of any kind, even a canteen of water.

The bland fare provided by Slater was the best meal she had ever tasted. There wasn't near enough of it, though. She was too proud, or stubborn, to ask Slater for second helpings. And she noticed that he offered nothing to the Apache girl, who sat as far away from Slater as the rope tied to both their waists would permit.

"Aren't you going to give her something to eat?" Amanda asked.

Slater looked at her, surprised. This was the first time since leaving the reservation that she had spoken.

"Waste of time," he replied. "She won't take anything from us."

"How do you know? You haven't offered."

"She's Apache. And she's a captive. She won't take any food or water while she's held against her will. She's like a few mustangs I've seen. Once caught, they'll go without graze or water until they die. You have to cut 'em loose if you want 'em to live. They won't bow under."

Amanda acted like she hadn't heard a word.

"You can't know that for a fact because you haven't tried."

Slater sighed. He got up and took a slice of dried beef to Chuana, hunkered down in front of the Apache girl and held the food out.

Chuana turned her head away.

Slater returned to where he'd been sitting before, impaled Amanda with a cold glare and muttered, "Women!"

Miffed, Amanda went to her horse and started to untie her blankets from back of the cantle— blankets that had once been the "hot roll" of Wink Langley's hostler, Jesus.

"What are you doing?" asked Slater.

"What does it look like?"

"Don't. We're not staying here."

"What?"

"We're not camping here," said Slater through gritted teeth.

Sure enough, after filling his canteen and watering the horses, Slater had them on their way again an hour later, shortly after moonrise. Ten miles from the rock tank, he finally called it a night.

"You don't camp at a waterhole that everybody and their dog knows about," Slater told her.

At the end of the second day they reached a mountain range. Passing through a narrow canyon, they emerged into a fertile valley thick with jackpine and aspen. After days of dust, rock and cactus, Amanda was infatuated with the hidden valley. Slater led them up a steep slope, a long and exhausting climb. When they finally stopped, thousands of feet above the lush floor of the valley, Amanda's leg muscles were so knotted that she wondered if she would ever walk again.

As he had done the night before, Slater unsaddled both horses, brushed them down, then put the saddles back on, leaving the cinches slightly loosened. One sharp tug on the latigos would screw the hull down tight. He massaged their legs and checked their hooves for splits and stones.

Leaving his gun and shellbelt hanging on the biscuit of his saddle, he went to Chuana and untied her hands. This he had also done the previous night. Chuana watched his face, with no expression on her own. Slater did not look her in the eye as he rubbed her hands and wrists to get the blood circulating again. He still felt ashamed for abducting her.

In short order, Chuana's hands were again bound.

Slater was shaking out his blankets when Amanda said, "You should let her go."

"No."

"This isn't right. What you're doing to her is just what Chacon did to me."

"Not exactly."

"You know what I mean."

"You want Chacon dead, don't you?"

Amanda looked over at Chuana. The moon had set. The night was pitch dark, and there was no fire—Slater wouldn't allow it—but she thought she could see the Apache girl's eyes blazing from twenty feet away.

"Yes," she said finally. "I still do. At first because of what he did to me. I knew what happened to white women who'd been . . . *taken* by Indians, once they got back to their own kind. I could see it in my father's eyes. I was . . . dirty. It would never be the same. I could never hold my head up and look anybody in the eye, for fear that I would see that same look. I was too humiliated. I thought I would prefer death to living like that."

"You don't feel that way any more?"

"Oh, I don't know. What I do know is that I want Chacon to pay for murdering Cameron."

"You and this Cameron feller. Close?"

"We were . . . friends."

"I reckon more than friends."

"All right. Yes. More than friends. We . . . I am sure that we would have been married."

Slater couldn't see tears, but he was fairly certain that Amanda, in a quiet way, was shedding some.

"Still, revenge, then," he said. "Just a different reason."

"I feel sorry for her. I can't believe I'm sitting here, so close to her, and wishing her father dead."

"She'd understand."

"What?"

"Apaches understand vengeance. They expect it from their enemies. They practice it, too."

"Which is why you know Chacon will come. Not just to save his daughter, but also to kill you for taking her."

"He'll die trying."

For a long moment they were silent, the only sound made by the wind howling through the craggy peaks high above them, and whispering through the boughs of the jackpine below.

"Listen," said Slater. "If you get a chance to kill Chacon, think of it this way. You'll be doing him a favor, not to mention yourself, as he will surely kill you if you hesitate. Apaches like him—and all the renegades with him—they've decided that they don't care to die locked up on some reservation. They want to die with honor, free to roam, with gun in hand, in a fight to the death. That's the way an Apache is meant to die. That's the way Chuana would want to remember her father."

They spoke no more.

Late the next day, they reached Diablo.

CHAPTER 24

THE SHEER, SANDSTONE CLIFFS RISING from the cactus flats were painted with scarlet and ochre shades of sunset. Try as she might, Amanda could see no way through this massive wall of stone, this giant, natural barricade ten miles wide. But Slater rode straight at the cliffs.

He knew exactly where to go. Hidden from view of anyone on the desert floor was a tent-shaped crevice, concealed behind huge boulders standing side-by-side. Through this narrow opening they passed, into an equally narrow canyon steeped in purple shadow.

The canyon, cooled by wind fluting through its

upper reaches, was a blessed relief from the punishing heat of the flats. There was scarcely enough room for them to pass. The entire way Amanda could have stretched out her arms and touched both walls at the same time. Had she looked straight up she might have occasionally glimpsed a sliver of darkening sky.

Instead, she paid full attention to her riding, and kept a tight grip on reins and saddlehorn. The floor of the tenuous passage was slick stone, and the horses had difficulty with their footing. She expected any minute to go down with the sorrel. In these close confines, such an accident would surely result in damage to horse or rider, or both.

On and on they went, until Amanda began to have the sensation of being buried alive under tons of rock. She also got the sense that they were climbing even higher, although the incline was always subtle.

Eventually they emerged onto a ledge. Here Slater paused, scanning the vast basin before him. Amanda was astonished by the sight. She was also leery of the sheer drop from the ledge to the floor of the basin, hundreds of feet below.

"Is this it?" she asked, breathless. "Is this Diablo?"

Slater nodded, ice-blue eyes sweeping the high jagged peaks encircling the basin. Steep slopes of loose shale and boulders angled downward from the bases of these peaks. The bottom of the basin was thick with jackpine and cedar, interspersed with great, open patches of slab rock. The sun had already dipped low behind the western heights. Shafts of blood-hued light lanced through cracks and crevices and played against the forbidding stone facade of the east rim. Up there, the shadows were alive and moving.

It was an eerie place, with a harsh and desolate aura that Amanda was sensitive to. Still and lifeless, like an immense stone tomb. Behind her, the wind fluting through the narrows sounded like the wailing of lost souls.

Somehow she knew, with utter conviction, that many had died here, and none lived here.

"Why do they call it Diablo?"

"Mexicans do, mostly," he replied. "Couple of times, their troops chased Apache raiders in here. We're right on the border. None of the soldiers ever came out alive. It's a death trap, lady. Custom made by Mother Nature. Only way in or out is the canyon we come through. Oh, I reckon you *could* climb out, if you had plenty of time, the strength of a mountain goat, and more luck than any one person had the right to expect."

"If it's a trap, why would the Apaches come here?"

"They don't much like to, unless there's no

help for it. This is haunted ground, in their opinion."

"Haunted?"

Slater pointed. "Look yonder."

She looked, to the far side of the basin, the north side, and for the first time saw the ruins.

They were easily overlooked. Made as they were from yellow sandstone bricks and adobe, and built beneath a massive ledge that cut deeply into the slopes, they looked to be an integral part of the landscape. She saw towers, several stories high, and deep, round pits, and chambers built on top of chambers. All the roofing had collapsed, and many of the walls were crumbling. But once it had been a great city. Amanda admired the craft of the people who had built it.

"Apache say the cliff-dwellers were the Ancient Ones, the Anasazi, their ancestors," said Slater. "This was one of their strongholds. They're long gone now. The Apache believe that the spirits of the Ancient Ones still roam here. So they generally steer clear. Unless they're being chased hard. Fact is, one or two good men with rifles and plenty of ammunition could hold that canyon back there against a whole army."

Amanda glanced at Chuana. The Apache girl looked apprehensive.

"If there's only one way in or out, though," said Amanda, striving to keep the anxiety she felt out of her voice, "and we've arrived before the Apache, then *we're* the ones who are trapped."

Slater's look was hard. "A trap's no good without bait."

"And we're the bait," she said softly.

He heeled the claybank into motion.

The ledge continued on around the eastern side of the basin, almost a mile in length, before reaching the vicinity of the cliff dwellings. Slater let his horse pick its way, for the ledge was narrow, sometimes precariously so.

The first stars flickered in the sky. Amanda decided before long that she preferred the cold oppression of the canyon to this dangerous traverse, where one false step spelled certain death.

Above the ledge, and below, there was either a sheer drop or an impossibly steep slope of shale debris. To fall down a slope was as lethal as plummeting off a cliff. Smashed into a bloody pulp or buried beneath an avalanche of rocks—there was little to choose between the two alternatives.

Amanda kicked her feet out of the stirrups and kept a white-knuckled grip on the biscuit of her saddle. If the sorrel stumbled, she was primed to at least try to jump clear and land on the ledge.

When she heard the clatter of small stones cascading down the shale slope ahead, Amanda's heart leaped into her throat. Her first thought was that an avalanche was about to sweep them all from the ledge and to their deaths.

Slater had a different first thought. There was a scattering of large boulders jutting out of the talus on the slope above them. Perfect hiding places for an ambusher—even half a hundred ambushers. A carelessly placed foot by someone concealed up there could have triggered the downward trickle of stones.

His hand dropped to the Schofield on his hip.

Something arced through the air above and in front of him. Before he had even identified the object, the revolver was drawn, cocked, aimed and fired. What looked like a short length of rope suddenly separated into two pieces.

At the same time, Chuana threw herself sideways, falling off the horse.

The two pieces of what looked like rope landed on the ledge only a few feet in front of the claybank. Slater had a split second to see that it was not rope, but a diamondback rattler. The snake had been cut clean in half by his shot. Both halves were still squirming, and the rattle on the rear half was going great guns.

The claybank, desert born and bred, knew all about diamondbacks. Snorting fear and hatred, the horse reared up on hind legs. Sharp, front hooves were its only weapons.

Chuana hit the ground. There was still plenty

of slack in the rope tied around both her waist and Slater's, so that Slater was not dragged from the saddle. But as the claybank reared, it placed a hind leg carelessly close to the rim of the ledge. Loose stone crumbled and gave way. The horse let out a shrill whinny. Slater jumped as the claybank lost its balance and went over the edge.

Slater's hurried leap was not graceful, and he landed painfully. A gun spoke, the booming report bouncing back and forth between the high peaks. He looked upslope, saw three men burst from cover behind those scattered boulders, and begin a rapid descent to the ledge. He knew all three.

Gault, Digby and Taggert.

Taggert tried to stop and fire his Sharps-Borschardt a second time, but his feet slipped out from under him just as he drew a bead on Slater. He fell and rolled in a small avalanche.

Slater got to his knees, put the Schofield right up to the rope that tied Chuana to him, and pulled the trigger. The rope came apart.

On her hands and knees a few feet away, Chuana fastened the eyes of a hunted doe upon him.

"Chuana," he rasped. "*Ugashe! Callate.* Run! Quick."

But there was nowhere to run. Digby had reached the ledge behind them, sliding the last twenty feet down the slope on his butt. He got up and shuffled forward in a flat-footed run, scattergun in hand. A second later, Ben Gault made the ledge ahead of them.

Unable to turn, Amanda's sorrel bolted straight ahead.

Both Chuana and Slater threw themselves to the slope-side of the high ledge to avoid being run over. As the horse reached Gault, the big buckskin-clad bounty hunter lashed out and caught Amanda by the arm, plucking her effortlessly out of the saddle. The sorrel charged recklessly on up the ledge as Gault swung Amanda roughly to the ground.

Rough male hands laying hold of her snapped something inside Amanda. She came up fighting like a wildcat, clawing at Gault's face and screaming hoarsely. Gault was not one to put up with such nonsense for long. He hit her in the face with a full-swung fist. She went down, out cold.

Slater took stock of the situation.

He had one man behind him, one in front, and one on the slope directly above. There was no escape. And no cover. In a split second he figured the odds and made his decision.

He thought he could take at least one of the bastards with him.

That one had to be Ben Gault.

"Gault!" he yelled, turning, standing, bringing the Schofield to bear.

Gault had his Colt double-action .45 in hand.

As he spun away from Amanda to confront Slater, he could tell in a glance that Slater had him dead to rights—that he was a heartbeat away from death.

Slater saw the surprise on Gault's face. And, maybe, just a trace of fear. That was gratifying.

Taggert's big Sharps rolling-block boomed again.

Slater felt like he'd been hit square-on by a six-horse-hitch running flat out. The impact hurled him off the high narrow ledge and into empty space.

The last thing he heard as he fell was Ben Gault's jubilant laughter echoing through the desolate crags of Diablo.

CHAPTER 25

"YOU DID IT, TAGGERT!" HOLLERED DIGBY AS he came lumbering along the ledge to the spot where Slater had gone over. "You blew that bastard's light out, sure enough!"

The ex-sheriff of San Manuel was at first beside himself with relief. Slater was dead and he was alive to celebrate the occasion. That made his day.

When he peered down into the obscuring gloom that had gathered below in the basin, he was struck with a new and less cheering thought. Ben Gault strolled over, and Digby threw a querulous look at the bounty hunter.

"But how the hell are we gonna get down there to recover the body?"

"We'll wait till mornin'," drawled Gault, quite satisfied with the success of the ambush he had engineered.

"Mornin'? Slater's carcass is worth good money."

"He ain't goin' nowheres, Digby."

"But what if the wolves or coyotes carry off the body?"

"Ain't been no lobos or coyotes in Diablo since I can remember. No game to speak of at all. You worry too much."

"No game? Why the hell not?"

Gault shrugged, taking a long, squint-eyed look around.

"This just ain't a fit place for living things."

"What's that supposed to mean?"

"Place is haunted, some say."

Digby snorted. "Haunted?" He sounded derisive, but Gault caught him casting nervous glances this way and that.

Digby told himself that he didn't believe in ghosts and such. Still, he wished that night wasn't so quick to fall.

"You want to break your fool neck, go on and try to get down there in the dark," said Gault. "It's fine with me if you kill yourself. Makes my share that much bigger."

"You keep saying that," snapped Digby, suspicious. "We agreed that your share was gettin' out of jail. Don't forget."

Gault flashed a wolfish grin that made Digby's skin crawl, and turned away.

Now that he no longer had to worry about Sam Slater, Digby commenced to worrying about a new threat, Ben Gault. Gault was crooked enough to contemplate doing away with his partners when the time was right. That way, he'd collect all the reward money for Slater that was waiting up Montana way.

And if Gault managed somehow to kill Chacon, then he could cut a deal with the governor. In return for Chacon's carcass, he could persuade Woodbine to drop the murder charges that were fresh on the books against him.

Taggert was standing over the Apache girl, the barrel of his Sharps against her head. She was huddled on the ground, impassively watching every move made by the three men.

Reaching down, Gault gathered up two handfuls of blanket-serape and yanked Chuana clean off her feet.

"Well now," leered Gault. "Ain't you a pretty little savage? I'm right proud to meet the daughter of the great Apache warrior, Chacon."

His face was very close to hers, and Chuana flinched at Gault's fetid breath.

The way Gault was holding her aloft, the blanket-serape was hiked up over the girl's buttocks. Taggert got an eyeful of soft, brown skin in the last light of the dying day.

"Hey, Gault," he muttered, his voice taut with lust. "Mebbe we should get better acquainted with her. What do you say?"

Gault grinned. "Don't see no harm. What do you think about that, *nah-lin?*"

Chuana could not comprehend the words, but she understood the meaning well enough. Her response was to spit in Gault's face and kick him in the groin.

Gault let out a howl and dropped her.

As the bounty hunter whirled away, groping his crotch and doubling over, Chuana took off, running like a deer.

Taggert shouted alarm, and brought the Sharps to his shoulder.

Recovering quickly, Gault knocked the rifle aside. He started after Chuana, shaking out his whip, previously shoulder-slung. Taggert marveled at the man's speed, especially since he'd just been kicked in the *cajones.*

Flawlessly measuring the girl's speed and his own, and the distance between, Gault let fly with the bullwhacker's whip.

The rawhide snaked around one of Chuana's slim ankles and brought her down.

Gault started reeling her in like a hooked fish.

Taggert threw aside the Sharps and churned past Gault, pouncing on the girl. Growling like a rutting bull, he began to tear at the blanket-serape with one hand while attempting to fondle Chuana's breasts with the other.

Gault walked up and kicked Taggert in the ribs as hard as he could. Grunting as he labored to suck air, Taggert rolled over and curled up in a ball.

"What the hell!" he gasped. "You said. . . ."

"I know what I said. But this ain't the time nor the place."

Gault dragged Chuana to her feet, cuffed her around until she was barely conscious, blood leaking from her slack mouth, then tied her up with the twenty-foot whip. By this time, Taggert had managed to struggle to his feet, hugging himself. His color started coming back. Gault threw Chuana to him.

"Try to hold onto that 'til we get back to camp."

He turned and walked away along the ledge. Taggert hefted Chuana onto one shoulder and followed, pausing to retrieve his rifle.

Digby was standing over near the woman Gault had de-horsed and knocked cold. As Gault approached, Digby stared at him, a horrified look on his whiskered face.

"Jesus Henry Christ," was all Digby could say.

"What?" barked Gault. Still hurting, he was not in a good frame of mind.

"Do you know who this is?" screeched Digby.

"No, and I don't give a good goddamn. I got what I want."

"This . . . this is Amanda Woodbine. The daughter of the territorial governor."

Gault stared at the unconscious woman.

"Wonder why she was riding with Sam Slater?"

"This is not good," said Digby, in a panic. "What do we do now? We're all as good as dead. God help us, we. . . ."

"Shuddup," snarled Gault. "I don't care if she's the Queen of bloody England. She ain't leavin' Diablo alive. Her body'll never be found, Digby, so you just grab hold of your nerve and stop wetting your pants. Then you grab hold of her and come the hell on."

Gault stalked on by. Taggert trudged along after, carrying the Apache girl.

Digby entertained the notion of running for his life. He quickly dismissed it. Ben Gault would kill him, sure as hell was hot.

Moving like a man on his last, long walk to the gallows, Heck Digby got Amanda's limp body on his shoulder and shuffled after the others.

CHAPTER 26

WHEN SLATER OPENED HIS EYES AND looked up at a star-frosted sky, he concluded that he had to be one of the all-time biggest fools on God's good, green earth.

He had purely underestimated Ben Gault and Heck Digby.

Clearly, the two had struck a deal. Slater had thought all along that Gault was languishing in the San Manuel hoosegow. The only reason he wasn't had to be one Heck Digby.

I should have known Ben Gault was too coyote-smart to hang, thought Slater.

Had he known that Gault was on the prowl,

he would have arranged things differently. He would never have picked Diablo for the rendez-vous with Chacon.

Because Gault was one of the few white men who knew where Diablo was.

Slater knew because he had lived for years among the Apaches, and was familiar with all the old legends. Gault knew because he had once—some years back—tracked a renegade breed to this remote mountain fastness. Slater had also been on the breed's trail. That time, Gault had gotten to Diablo first.

And he had this time, too.

Muttering under his breath, Slater called himself every uncomplimentary name in the book. Meanwhile, he gingerly felt his side. His hand came away sticky with blood. The pain was immense. Felt like a red-hot iron rod had been run clean through him.

Teeth clenched, he poked and prodded with his fingers, and this time felt the deep groove, half-way between ribcage and hipbone, that Taggert's bullet had made. A few more inches and he'd have been gunshot, and dying now by slow and agoniz-ing degrees.

A fool, certainly. But a *lucky* fool.

He tested his body for broken parts, moving first one leg, then the other, then the other arm, his shoulders, neck and head. Everything was plenty sore, but all the bones were apparently intact. He turned his head slightly and studied the path of his descent from the ledge high above.

It was full night, and either too early or too late for the moon, he had no way of knowing which. But there was enough starlight to see by.

He thought he could tell where the ledge was, way up yonder, maybe two hundred feet above him. He had fallen over fifty feet straight down, struck a shale slope, and rolled the rest of the way. Now he was lodged against a rock outcropping. He was not anywhere near the bottom of the basin. The outcropping had caught him and kept him from falling farther. He had no idea if the shale slope continued all the way to the bottom or if there was another sheer drop-off on the other side of the outcropping.

Slater couldn't remember rolling. Just falling. So he must have knocked himself out hitting the top of the shale slope, or blacked out in mid-air. That was another lucky break. His body had been limp as he cartwheeled down the slope, which was why he hadn't broken anything.

The Apaches had taught him to let his body go slack when taking a fall, regardless of whether the fall was suffered in hand-to-hand combat or the result of being thrown by a horse. The same rule applied, apparently, when falling off a mountain.

Moving tentatively, he sat up against the outcropping, winced at the lancing pain that the slightest exertion caused.

He thought about the Schofield. A quick search revealed that the gun was not nearby. Scanning the shale slope, he accepted the fact that he would never find it in the dark.

This led him to wonder about the Spencer .56-50. The carbine had been in the saddle boot, and the saddle was still on the claybank. The horse lay dead about twenty yards to his right.

Slater felt a twinge of regret. The claybank had been a damned fine desert horse. He'd be hard put to find a replacement with as much bottom and savvy.

He wasted another couple of minutes in merciless self-criticism. He had blundered into Gault's ambush like a greenhorn. True, Gault had left no sign coming through the canyon—the route he must have taken into Diablo. It occurred to Slater that he wasn't the only hunter who knew how to use rawhide "boots" on the hooves of horses.

Gault had second-guessed him all the way. Deducing that Slater would go first to the Bedonkohe *rancheria* at Cibicu Creek, he had gone there himself, learned of Chuana's abduction and the arranged meet at Diablo. All this was now clear to Slater.

So Gault had Chuana. Slater didn't hold out much hope that the girl had escaped. Gault was planning to use Chuana in the same way Slater had intended to use her: as bait to lure Chacon into his gunsights.

That was bad enough: worse still was what Gault and the others might do to Chuana in the meantime.

Not to mention what they might do to Amanda Woodbine.

Slater accepted responsibility for Chuana. He told himself that Amanda really had only herself to blame for whatever befell her. After all, he hadn't invited her to tag along.

He told himself all that but he couldn't quite make himself believe it.

He began to work his way across the treacherous slope in the direction of the dead horse. It took him half an hour to negotiate those twenty yards. He had to stop frequently to rest and catch his breath and let the pain subside. Cold sweat poured out of him.

One fact became immediately clear: the rock outcropping had saved his bacon. There *was* another cliff below him. His lateral traverse of the slope sent a few stones bouncing over the edge. He counted slowly to five before hearing them hit bottom. That convinced him that it was quite a drop. Which, in turn, meant he had to climb *up* to get out of this fix.

He indulged in a little second-guessing of his

own. Gault and the others, like as not, figured him for dead. They would wait until daylight to come down and search for his body. Taggert's presence made it clear that they intended to collect the Montana reward for him. But they weren't apt to risk the dangerous slopes at night.

So he had to get the hell and gone from here before daybreak.

Reaching the claybank, he first pulled the Spencer carbine from its scabbard and checked it over from barrel to stock, making certain that it had not been damaged in the fall.

Next, he took a spare shirt from his saddlebags, tore it into long strips, and bound his midsection as tight as he could stand with this makeshift dressing. He would have to cauterize the wound as soon as possible, to remove the risk of infection. There was no way to accomplish that now, though.

For a while he sat there, braced against the bulk of the dead horse, studying the cliff above him, and trying to pick the best route for an ascent.

Part of him said that it just couldn't be done. Not in his condition. Slater ignored that part. That was the white man in him talking. The Apache in him said it didn't matter if it *could* be done, because it *had* to be done.

Part of the rope that had once tied Chuana to him was still secured around his waist. He worked the knot loose, and fashioned the rope into a sling for the Spencer. After taking a sip of water, he draped the canteen by its strap over his shoulder. There were extra rounds for the Spencer in his saddlebags, so he lashed these to the back of his gunbelt with a tie cut from the saddle with his clasp knife. Finally, he turned his bandanna into a head band to keep the hair out of his eyes. He had lost his hat in the fall.

He began to crawl up the shale slope. The incline was severe, and purchase in the loose shale was hard to come by. Several times the shale gave way and he slid down. Progress was agonizingly slow. He measured it in inches. Patience and persistence were his allies. He knew that to rush would ultimately send him tumbling over the cliff beneath him in an avalance of rocks.

The moon rose above the jagged peaks on the east rim during this, the first stage of his climb. It was nearing the west rim when he finally reached the base of the cliff from which he had fallen after being shot by Taggert.

Here he permitted himself a long rest. His hands were sore and bleeding from digging in the shale. His pants were torn at the knees, and he could feel blood running down his legs. His side hurt like hell. He refused to let the pain dictate to him. He also refused to entertain any doubt that he could climb the sheer rock face to the ledge.

It's only fifty damned feet, give or take, he told himself.

Opening the clasp knife, he clenched it in his teeth, forced himself to his feet, and began the ascent.

Every foot was a challenge. The moon, over his shoulder, helped by illuminating the face of the cliff, accentuating every fissure and lip. Sometimes he used the knife to chip a handhold or foothold into the sandstone. He carefully tested every hold before trusting his weight to it.

Before long his hands began to ache, and then to cramp. The rasp of his labored breathing and the pounding of blood in his ears was all he could hear. He pushed himself mercilessly.

He reached the ledge.

With what he measured as his last ounce of strength, Slater started to drag himself over the rim.

He did not hear them coming. But he chanced to look left, and that's when he saw them, fifty yards away down the ledge, loping toward him on steel-muscled legs.

Apaches.

CHAPTER 27

SLATER WAS IN SUCH A HURRY TO DUCK down below the rim of the ledge that he almost lost his tenuous grip and fell.

He figured they had to have seen him. Apaches had the night vision of cats. Taking the clasp-knife from between his teeth, he prepared to hurl it at the first Indian who stuck his nose out over the edge.

Instead, he heard the soft tread of their desert moccasins as they ran on by.

Slater cautiously struggled back up and over the rim, looking after them in wonder.

The only explanation was that they knew there

were *Pinda-Lickoyi* somewhere up ahead, and they had no reason to suspect that one of them was dangling precariously from the cliff below them.

Looking in the opposite direction, toward the canyon entrance to Diablo, Slater saw no sign of more Apaches. Still, he knew they were there. The pair that had missed him had to be part of Chacon's raiding party. He had no doubts on that score. Back at Ghost Springs he had counted eight by the sign they had left at the site of the stage station attack.

Neither of the two he had just seen was Chacon. Slater was sure that they had been sent out in advance, to scout the basin. Chacon and the others were probably still back in the canyon. Chacon would be especially cautious entering Diablo, and would not cavalierly relinquish his hold on the only way out.

Resting a moment, Slater considered the odds as he worked the cramps out of his hands and leg muscles. A smart gambler would cash in with odds like these. But Slater couldn't walk away from this game.

He was alone against a band of Apache renegades, not to mention the firm of Gault, Digby and Taggert.

Only one thing to do. Start cutting down the odds.

He got up and began to run along the ledge,

in the wake of the two Apaches, knife in one hand, Spencer in the other.

In a matter of minutes, Slater caught up with the two Apaches.

They were running single-file, about ten feet apart. Both carried rifles.

He wasn't surprised that they had chosen to enter Diablo on foot. They could move more quickly and more quietly along the ledge this way than on horseback.

Slater wore desert moccasins, as did the Indians, and he made no more noise than they. He did his best to keep in stride with the rearmost Apache, so that his feet fell in unison with the Indian's. At the same time, he tried to lengthen his stride. That wasn't easy to do and stay in step, but it was the only way to close the gap. He concentrated most of all on his breathing, inhaling deeply and exhaling slowly to minimize the sound.

Sooner or later the Apaches would hear him, or sense his presence. Every foot closer before discovery improved his chances of survival. He'd been dancing with Lady Luck all night, and could only hope that the music played on just a little longer.

He was thirty feet from the rearmost Apache.

One uncertainty tormented him. He couldn't remember if there was a round in the Spencer's breech. If not, it would take him an extra second to fire. Up against Apaches, a single second could be the difference between life and death.

Twenty feet.

If he could avoid any shooting at all, that would be good. Taking on Gault and company would be tough enough without their being alerted by gunfire.

Ten feet.

He saw the nearest runner's head begin to turn. Slater put on a burst of speed, throwing stealth to the wind.

Seeing Slater, the Apache whirled. He did not cry out an alarm. There was no need. The other Indian had also heard, and was also turning.

The nearest Apache had a repeater held at hip level, and was lining up his shot when Slater lashed out with his left hand, slashing at the renegade's face with the clasp-knife even as he dodged to one side.

Slater's blade cut deeply. A warm spray of blood struck him as he swept past the now-falling Apache. He collided with the second runner. There wasn't time to check for certain that the first one was out of the fight.

The second Apache managed to crouch low before Slater hit him, so that Slater's impetus carried him onto the Indian's back. The Apache heaved upright, hurling the bounty hunter head-over-heels. Slater landed at the rim of the ledge.

He felt the stone crumble and give way beneath him. Letting go of the Spencer, he groped desperately for a hold.

For one breathless instant he was suspended on the very brink, fighting gravity, clawing for life.

The Apache saved him.

That wasn't the Indian's intent. Leaping forward, he kicked out, hoping to send Slater plummeting to his death. But Slater latched onto the extended leg with both hands. He felt himself going over and tightened his bulldog grip on the Apache. The Apache twisted and dropped to flatten himself on the ledge. Slater climbed up his leg. The Indian sat up and slammed a fist into Slater's face. Slater spat blood and kept climbing. The Apache grasped the knife in his belt. Safely on the ledge now, Slater rolled away.

He rolled over a rifle, and came up with the barrel in both hands. A Henry repeater, the Apache's weapon, dropped during the collision.

The Indian leaped to his feet and lunged, slashing with the knife. Slater ducked underneath the swing and slammed the rifle into the Apache's knees. The stock cracked. The bronco went down. Slater drove the rifle, butt-first, into the Apache's face. The stock splintered. Again Slater struck. The runner's face dissolved into a bloody pulp. His body went rigid, heels drumming as legs spasmed. Then he was still.

Slater rose, the shattered rifle in hand, looked up to see the other Apache staggering towards him. His cheek was laid open to the bone. One eye had been destroyed. His forehead was gashed to the hairline. Slater could see skullbone through the grotesque mask of blood and torn flesh. There was so much blood that it was getting into the Indian's remaining eye and effectively blinding him. He had lost his rifle; unable to find it, he was moving to the sound of fighting with knife in hand.

Slater backed away. The Apache stumbled and fell over the body of his fallen comrade. He picked himself up and came on. Slater felt a surge of admiration for this one. A true warrior. Disabled, but still deadly.

"*Netdahe.* Wild One," said Slater softly. "Over here."

Snarling, the Apache lunged. Slater struck the knife away with what was left of the rifle. The Indian lost his balance. Slater stepped in and hammered the renegade between the shoulder blades with an arm locked rigid.

The Apache vanished over the edge.

He made no cry as he fell. Slater hadn't expected him to.

The bounty hunter sent what was left of the Henry sailing out over the cliff. He pushed the other body over the edge, and the other Apache rifle. He found the Spencer. The clasp-knife eluded him, so he confiscated one of the Chiricahua blades.

He checked the site, thoroughly. If anyone passed by in the darkness, and did not look too closely, they would not know what had occurred here. Daylight would reveal the blood and scuffed rock. But Slater was confident that by daybreak everything would be resolved. One way or another.

Weapons in both hands, he ran on through the night, along the ledge, in the direction of the ancient cliff dwellings.

CHAPTER 28

HECK DIGBY REFLECTED, WITH ENORMOUS self-pity, that never in his misspent life had he been in worse need of mescal in strong dosage.

Problem was, he'd killed his last bottle many miles ago.

This was the worst possible time to suffer enforced sobriety. For one thing, he did not like sitting in the rubble of one of the cliff-dwellings. This place beat all he had ever seen. It was downright spooky. A fire would have been some small comfort, but Gault had forbidden a fire, so Digby huddled in the gloom of deep night, nervously clutching his scattergun, cutting his eyes at the big gap in the wall that led to the outside.

The horses stood with heads together on the other side of the chamber. One of them nickered softly, and Digby almost jumped out of his skin. He decided then and there that he would gladly forsake all the reward money in the world just to be back in his rocker in front of the San Manuel jail.

From a dark corner, Amanda said, "Cut me loose, Sheriff. We're both running out of time."

"I ain't a sheriff no more, dammit," groused Digby.

Peer as hard as he might, he could scarcely see her in the darkness. She was tied hand and foot, though, so he wasn't worried about her slipping away.

"You're not like them," she said. Her voice was calm. Digby envied her. For a woman in her predicament, Amanda Woodbine was acting mighty hard-shelled.

"Shuddup." It came out more a plea than a command.

"I can help you get out of this."

Digby snorted. "You're the one needin' help."

"There'll be no help for you, Heck Digby, if you stay with the others."

"Just shut the hell up."

"You know my father would do anything I ask

of him. I can get him to wipe the slate clean, as far as you're concerned."

"Too late," muttered Digby, disconsolate. He sounded like a man with the noose already around his neck.

Amanda gave up on him. She glanced at the odd, T-shaped doorway set into one wall. It led to an adjoining chamber. Some time ago, Gault and Taggert had dragged the Apache girl through that doorway. For a while Amanda had heard the brutal and disgusting sounds of their lust. Not once had Chuana cried out. Now the room beyond the doorway was deathly quiet.

She feared the worst.

A shadow moved in the doorway. Ben Gault. He looked sated and disheveled, and was wiping the blade of a scalphunter's knife on the sleeve of his grime-blackened shirt. The whip he had previously used to bind Chuana was coiled on a shoulder.

"You bastard," said Amanda, quietly.

Teeth flashed as he grinned at her.

Digby stood up, moving like a sleepwalker.

"What have you done, Gault?"

"Oh, did you want some, Digby? You should've stepped right up and said so. A little late, now."

Taggert came through the doorway. He stumbled and caught himself, looking back into the dense darkness of the adjacent chamber, then at

Gault's back. His expression told the story. He looked like he was going to puke.

"Lord A'mighty," breathed Digby, shaken to the core. "You killed her, didn't you, Gault? And then you lifted her hair."

"Why not? You can still get good money for Apache scalps down south. What do you care anyhow, Digby? She was just a dirty Cherry Cow savage. Chacon's gonna come, whether she's dead or alive."

Amanda laughed.

All three men were startled, and a bit unnerved. There was something strangely off-key about her laughter.

Gault struck without warning, backhanding her. He cocked his arm back for another blow. Amanda tossed tangled golden hair out of her eyes and looked up at him. Blood trickled from a split lip. Her eyes betrayed no fear.

"Somethin' funny, lady?" growled Gault.

"You. Calling her a 'dirty savage.'"

Grabbing her arm in a vise-like grip, he yanked her to her feet, put his face real close to hers.

"You sayin' I'm no better than a stinkin' Apache bitch?"

Amanda did not flinch. She saw everything in a new light, a light that cast no shadows.

Slater had been right all along. She had been

wrong to hate all Apaches for what a few renegades had done to her. Apaches weren't all animals. Some were good, some were bad. Same could be said for white men.

She realized, too, that out here a woman had to think like a man and fight like a man if she wanted to survive. A woman was a gold-plated fool to expect any special consideration because of her gender. She remembered her righteous outrage when Slater had jumped her on the banks of Prospect Creek. Now she understood that in his own rough way Slater had been trying to tell her that if she persisted in acting like a woman she would continue to be a victim.

Amanda Woodbine was through playing the victim.

"I'm saying you're a sorry excuse for a man," she told Gault.

He hurled her roughly to the ground.

"Mebbe I should show you just what kind of man I am," he growled.

She rolled over on her back. He was standing over her, the scalping knife clenched in one massive fist.

"You're a big, tough hombre, aren't you?" she taunted defiantly. "Why don't you untie me, and we'll see just how tough you really are?"

Gault snickered.

"You'd like that, wouldn't you? So's you could try and run."

"I'm not going to run. I'm going to kill you."

This kind of talk from a woman was a new experience for Ben Gault. He glanced with a dazed half-grin at Digby and Taggert. Neither appeared inclined to advise him on how to deal with this novel situation.

Hot rage came to the boil in Gault. The fact that this woman was not terrified of him—that she dared to challenge him this way—damaged his ego.

Snarling, he dropped to his knees, pushed her over onto her face and used the knife to cut the rope binding her ankles and wrists together.

"You want to fight? You go ahead and fight. Kick and scratch all you want." He stood up and stepped back into a knife-fighter's crouch. "Come on. Get the hell up. I'm gonna enjoy this. That Apache girl, she just lay there and took it. Didn't move. Didn't make a sound. I reckon this'll be a lot more entertainin'."

Amanda rose slowly, rubbing her wrists. She stood there, in the midst of these three desperate men, her head down, her hair a yellow veil hiding her face.

Gault's laugh began as a low rumbling, building into a wall-shaking crescendo. He threw back his head and howled like a mad dog, his guffaws echoing through the ruins.

"Jesus, Gault!" snapped Digby crossly. "Keep a lid on it, will ya?"

Seeing her chance, Amanda jumped Digby.

She got both hands on the barrel of the sawed-off shotgun. Digby, expecting her to try jerking the weapon out of his grasp, pulled back on it sharply. Instead, Amanda shoved with all her might, driving the Davenport's stock into the man's paunch. The air whooshed! out of Digby. He fell backward over rubble. Amanda twisted the scattergun out of his grasp as he went down.

She spun as Gault lunged at her. She pulled one trigger. The shotgun spat flame. The double-aught kicked the big man off his feet. She saw Taggert move, and pivoted, letting go with the other barrel. The greener kicked like a bay steer. The buckshot peppered the wall above and behind Taggert, who had dropped into a crouching stance as he reached for the Remington Navy Model in his holster.

"Hey you," said Slater.

Taggert's head jerked around.

Slater was standing in the gap formed when half of one of the walls had crumbled.

Taggert uttered a strangled cry and carried on with his draw.

Slater fired the Spencer, worked the loading

lever and fired again. The .50 caliber slugs punched Taggert backward. The Remington hadn't even cleared leather. Taggert hit the wall, slipping down into a sitting position, then tipping over, dead eyes staring blankly.

Hearing Digby scrambling, Amanda whirled and raised the empty scattergun as she would a club. Slater reached her and snatched the Davenport out of her hands. She turned on him, eyes spitting fire.

"Go quiet the horses," he said flatly.

She stifled an angry retort, gave a curt nod, and crossed the chamber to the horses, who were reacting to the sudden whirlwind of violence by trying to break free of their tethers.

Slater turned on Digby, who was plastered against a wall, his face an alabaster-white oval in the darkness, his body trembling in a paroxysm of sheer terror. Slater sniffed. More than the rancid stench of fear came off Digby. San Manuel's ex-sheriff had voided his bowels.

"For the love of God," whined Digby. "Don't kill me, Slater."

"You said there'd be a time and a place for us to settle our differences. Won't this time and place do?"

"I'm, I'm unarmed, Slater! Jesus, you wouldn't shoot an unarmed man, would you?"

Slater's smile was bleak. "Why not? Wouldn't you?"

"Slater! Look out!"

Amanda's warning coincided with the lethal whisper of rawhide. The whip sliced through Slater's shirt and cut deeply into his back.

Roaring, Gault lumbered into Slater. Both men went down. The Spencer clattered on stone. Slater kicked both legs up and threw Gault over his head. When he came up he had the Apache knife in hand. Rising, Gault glanced at the blade, a silver flicker in the gloom, and laughed.

"I'll kill you with my bare hands," he snarled, throwing the bullwhip away. "I'll squeeze your skull 'til. . . ."

"You crazy sonuvabitch," said Slater. "I've heard all that before."

His bearded face an ugly brutal mask, Gault charged.

Slater stood his ground and took the full impact. Gault hit him like a boulder rolling downhill, and Slater landed on his back twenty feet from where he'd been standing, with Gault's full weight coming down hard on top of him. Twisting the knife that was buried to the hilt in Gault's midsection, Slater felt the gush of hot blood on his hand and arm, soaking through his clothes.

Grunting with the effort, Slater pushed Gault's slack body away, withdrawing the knife, and straddled the big man's barrel chest. Gault wasn't all the way dead. He clutched Slater's throat with one hand. Iron fingers squeezed.

"I'll snap your neck like I would a dry. . . ."

He heaved and spat blood.

One quick slash and Slater laid his throat open with the Apache blade.

Gault's grip loosened. Knocking the arm away, Slater stood up.

A gunshot spun him around.

He saw Amanda first, with Taggert's Remington gripped in both hands. He followed the direction of her rock-steady aim and watched Digby, silhouetted in the gap, keel slowly forward and fall dead.

"He was getting away," she explained, her voice dull.

"He wouldn't have gotten far."

"What do you mean?"

"Chacon's here."

Amanda lowered the smoking gun.

"Didn't waste any time, did he? But he's too late, just the same."

"Too late?"

"She's dead." Amanda nodded at the T-shaped doorway to the next chamber.

Feeling suddenly very tired, Slater grimly went through the doorway to see for himself.

A pocket search turned up a strike-anywhere.

He flicked the match to life with his thumbnail. One glance was all he needed to verify Amanda's statement. There was no point in checking for a pulse. He didn't want to get that close, anyway. He knew death well enough to recognize it, even at this distance in the dark.

Chuana's murder hit him hard. An innocent girl was dead, and he was solely to blame.

"I'm sorry," he muttered, and blew out the match.

He returned to the other chamber. Amanda was seated on a large sandstone block, leaning back against the wall, the Remington in her lap. Taggert's corpse, within reach, did not seem to bother her in the least.

"When will Chacon come?" she asked, not a trace of fear evident in voice or features.

Retrieving the Spencer, he sat down beside her, laid his head back against the wall, closed his eyes, and said, "At daybreak."

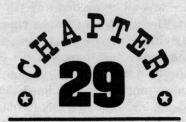

CHAPTER 29

AMANDA WAS SLEEPING PEACEFULLY WHEN Slater shook her gently awaken.

"Chacon's here," he said.

Gray shreds of light were creeping through the ruins. She heard nothing. Diablo was deathly still. No Apache war cries, no gunfire. No evidence at all that anything was wrong.

She looked up into his face. Pure impulse drove her to reach out and touch the scar that snaked across his burnished cheek.

"How did that happen?"

The question caught him off guard. This hardly seemed the appropriate time for small talk.

"A long story," he replied gruffly. "I'll tell you later."

For some reason, his evasion hurt her. He changed his mind. There probably wouldn't be a "later," anyway.

"The man I killed in Montana gave it to me. He was my uncle. We got into a fight when he tried to rape my cousin. He lost the fight."

Her eyes held a light that was both soft and bright. "You're not such a bad man after all, Sam Slater."

He stood up, went to the horses, took the rolled blanket from behind one of the saddles, and carried it into the next chamber. A moment later he emerged, with Chuana's body, wrapped in the blanket, cradled in his arms. The Spencer hung by its rope sling down his back.

"What are you going to do?" she asked, rising.

"Chacon came for his daughter. I'm going to give him what he came for."

He started for the breach in the wall.

"You can't just walk out there," she protested. "They'll kill you."

He pointed with his chin. "Take a look."

She moved cautiously to the breach and looked outside.

A few yards from the wall was one of the deep circular pits. On the far side of the pit sat Chacon. He appeared to be alone, sitting cross-legged, back rigid, gazing down into the pit. A Winchester lay across his lap. He wore only *n'deh b'keh* and breechclout, and a blue bandanna for a headband.

She turned on Slater. "Why don't you shoot him?"

"Why don't you? Isn't that what you came for?"

She glanced at the bodies of Gault and Taggert and Digby. Searching her heart, she found not a trace of the need for vengeance which had sustained her throughout the ordeal of the past week.

"I don't care about that anymore. I'm sorry."

"For what?"

"For my father and I getting you into this. Making you do what you didn't want to do. But we did, and now you must kill that man out there."

"Yes, I must. Stay here."

He went on by, climbed through the gap, stepping over Digby's body.

High above, in the cloudless sky, buzzards were already circling. Pink shades of sunrise painted the faces of the peaks on the western rim of Diablo. Shadows of night yet huddled in the bottom of the basin, a hundred yards below the ledge hosting the cliff dwellings.

He stopped at the rim of the pit opposite Chacon, twenty feet away from the Apache raider.

Chacon slowly lifted his gaze. His eyes were dark, fierce slits. His broad nose hooked like a hawk's beak above a knife-slash mouth. High-boned cheeks looked like flat sheets of copper. No expression softened these harsh features as he looked upon the blanket-wrapped body in Slater's arms.

"*Chikisin*," said Slater, "here is your daughter."

He laid Chuana down gently, and remained on one knee.

"Scar calls Chacon brother. Would one brother come into another's camp and steal his flesh-and-blood?"

"We all do what we have to do."

Chacon nodded. "That is true. No matter who is hurt. Chacon did what he had to when he left the agency and made war against the *Pinda-Lickoyi*. This he had to do because his spirit was dying. He did it, knowing that his war would bring much trouble to the Bedonkohe Chiricahua." He stared at the blanket-wrapped body. "Scar was never Chacon's brother. He was always just another white-eyes. But he would not do this."

"No. The men who did are dead. But Scar is to blame. He might as well have driven the knife into her body."

Chacon rose in one quick, fluid motion. He circled the rim of the pit. Slater stood, but did not back away. A moment later they were standing face-to-face.

"What must Scar do now?"

"He lured Chacon here to kill him."

Once more Chacon glanced at the body lying between them. "That has been done."

Slater made his choice. "Go on. Get the hell out of here."

The Apache warrior gave Slater a long study. It seemed to the bounty hunter that Chacon understood exactly what was going on here. That only extreme circumstances could have compelled Slater to break his vow never to hunt the Apache and that he would never have stolen Chuana from Cibicu Creek except to save his own life.

And now Slater was risking his life by letting Chacon go in peace.

Slater bent, picked up Chuana's body, and transferred it to Chacon's arms. Then he took a step back.

"No more killing," said Chacon. "This Apache will not be seen again. *Yadalanh*, Scar."

Yadalanh, goodbye of a permanent nature. Slater drew from this that Chacon's war with the white-eyes was over.

For himself, Slater was already making new plans. He would leave this country forever, running far and fast. Maybe, just maybe, he could lose himself in Mexico. He would live the life of a wanted man, if such could be called living. But at least he would not have to kill his Apache brother.

He owed his Apache father, Loco, that much.

As Chacon turned away, Slater felt a great weight lifted from his shoulders.

The renegade leader was on the other side of the pit, near where he had been sitting earlier. He suddenly fell to his knees, setting Chuana's body down, and twisted to face Slater.

Slater saw the Winchester sweeping around, watched in disbelief as Chacon thumbed the hammer back.

"No, brother!"

Even as he yelled, Slater was moving, dodging sideways, pulling the Spencer off his shoulder.

This time he knew for a fact that there was a round in the breach.

He fired, a fraction of a second before Chacon.

His bullet drilled the Apache's heart, flinging him backward. Chacon sprawled over the body of his daughter, dead instantly.

Hearing a boot scrape rock behind him, Slater whirled, crouching, working the carbine's lever action.

"Throw it down, Slater."

Blane. The man who had been with Amanda Woodbine in Doc Holzer's store that night back in San Manuel. The governor's personal bodyguard and a territorial marshal to boot. He was just as Slater remembered him. The long, black slicker.

The low-crowned hat shading the eyes of a hunter. The bladed nose and thick mustache.

He stood on top of a wall high above, and he had his Colt sidegun aimed rock-steady at Slater.

"Much obliged," he said. "That Apache's bullet missed me by a hair. I guess you saved my life."

"We all make mistakes," said Slater.

CHAPTER 30

SLATER REALIZED THAT CHACON HADN'T been gunning for him, after all, but for Blane.

The sound of horses drew his gaze away from the territorial marshal. He spotted the single-file column of blue-coated riders on the ledge that connected Diablo's canyon entrance to the cliff dwellings.

"That'll be Captain Mack and his buffalo soldiers," said Blane. He jumped to a lower intersecting wall, then dropped to the ground with the agility of a man in fighting trim. He walked toward Slater with the Colt held down by his side. Slater took it as a bad sign that Blane wasn't ready to holster his gun.

Amanda appeared in the breach of the chamber wall. Recognizing Blane, she lowered Taggert's Remington. Blane touched his hat brim.

"Miss Woodbine. I'm right relieved to see you alive and well."

"I am. Thanks to Mr. Slater."

Blane gave Slater a funny look. "Your father sent me out after you, ma'am. I have to admit, you made me look bad, slipping away like you did at Langley's place. The governor made it plain that if I didn't bring you back safe and sound, then I wasn't to come back at all."

"I'm safe. There are three dead men over here. They kidnapped me. Mr. Slater rescued me."

"Did he now? That would be Ben Gault, Heck Digby and that feller Taggert, I guess."

"How did you know?"

"It's a long story." Blane walked right up to Slater, looked him squarely in the eye. "I tracked you to Prospect Creek, ma'am. You met up with somebody there. Lost the trail after that, but it pointed to Cibicu Creek, so I went on there. Found out what Slater had done. Also found the tracks of three riders. One had to be Heck Digby. I knew that because of the empty mescal bottles. So I figured another was Gault, as Gault disappeared from jail the same night Digby cut out of San Manuel. The third had to be Taggert, because he and Digby had been up to something. So I followed them down here. Run across Captain Mack and his soldiers yesterday. They'd been chasing Chacon to hell and back. Pardon the language, Miss Woodbine."

"I've heard worse, believe me."

Blane brushed past Slater, circled the pit. He stood looking down at Chacon's body.

"You beat me to it, Slater. Looks like you collect the five thousand dollars."

"Didn't know you were after the bounty, too."

"I wasn't. It's my job to hunt down wanted men—and kill them, if necessary."

He looked at Slater again, and Slater began to wonder if this man knew, somehow, about Montana. It was an unhappy thought.

Amanda crossed the hardpack to Slater's side.

"What happened to the other Apaches, Mr. Blane?"

"We captured three of them, ma'am. Killed two others. That was last night. They were making for the tall timber away from this place. One of the prisoners talked to a Coyotero scout. Admitted that they'd had a falling out with Chacon. Seems two of their friends went in here and never came back out. Then they heard gunfire. They figured it was a trap, and were dead set against coming in.

So Chacon told them to go ahead and vamoose. They ran smack into our camp, just about."

"Apaches won't follow their *jefe* if they don't trust his judgment," said Slater.

Blane nodded. "I reckon Chacon's judgment was some clouded."

"He did what he had to."

Blane hunkered down, lifted a corner of the blanket to have a look at Chuana's face.

"This must be what he came for. The girl you stole from Cibicu Creek, Slater. Mister, you sure stirred up the nest. When all the dust clears, you might be facing charges."

"No, he won't," said Amanda.

Both men looked at her in surprise.

"He was trying to save her life. Gault and the others were going to kidnap her themselves. They were after Chacon, too. Mr. Slater knew she wouldn't be safe at the agency. He was trying to get her to Chacon. But Gault and the others ambushed us. They took the girl. Then they killed her."

"That's quick thinking, ma'am," congratulated Blane.

"I don't much care for what you're implying," she snapped, hot under the collar. "Did you, or did you not, see the tracks of those three men at Cibicu Creek?"

"Yes, ma'am. I just finished saying that I did."

"Well, then. That's what I'm going to tell my father. Do you think he'll believe me?"

Blane holstered his gun.

"Yes, ma'am. He'll believe whatever you tell him." He looked at Slater. "Guess I was wrong about those charges."

Slinging the Spencer over his shoulder, Slater left them without a word.

He fetched two of the horses from the chamber. Amanda would need the third. The sorrel she had lost during the ambush was running loose somewhere in Diablo.

Pulling the saddle off a roan gelding, he laid the bodies of Chacon and Chuana across the horse's back. The cavalry arrived, swirling dust across the ruins, as he finished lashing the bodies down with rope.

Captain Mack rode straight up to Slater. "What happened here?"

"Day late and a dollar short, as usual, Captain."

"Where are you going?"

Slater didn't think that was any of Mack's business, so he didn't answer.

"Let him go, Captain," advised Blane, an amused expression on his face as he looked sidelong at Amanda. "I have a hunch Slater's going to come out of this clean as a hound's teeth."

The officer slacked in his sweat-stained Mc-

Clellan saddle. He looked too bone-tired to argue the point.

"Maybe so," he conceded. "After all, he's got Chacon. He'll be some kind of hero in these parts."

Slater's smile was cold.

"Aren't any heroes out here, Captain."

He swung aboard the other horse, the reins of the roan gelding in his grasp. Amanda rushed forward, working her way through the dusty melee of curveting cavalry mounts.

"You're not going to collect the reward, are you?"

"No. Chacon told me his war was over. That he would not be seen again. He won't be. I won't have his body put on public display, for all the white-eyes to gawk at. My brother's going to some wild mountainside, up in the high lonesome, where he's free."

She smiled.

"You're not so bad, Sam Slater."

"Neither are you, Miss Woodbine."

He kicked the horse into motion. Passing through the cluster of Tenth Cavalry horse soldiers, he recognized the sergeant he had seen some days ago in the San Manuel cantina.

The three-striper gave a friendly nod.

Slater didn't acknowledge it.

He rode on past, onto the ledge, through the narrow canyon, and out of Diablo.

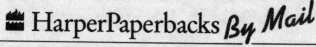